DREAMS OF THE PHILIPPINES

Dave Ives

This book is a work of fiction.

ISBN-13: 978-1540785299
ISBN-10: 1540785297

CONTENTS

PREFACE

This story is fiction. But it's based on a trip I took to the Philippines back in early 1989 as a young air-force second lieutenant.

This book represents a new step in my writing career. I'm venturing a little deeper into the world of fiction. What does that mean? Let me take a stab at explaining.

My previous two books—like this one—are fiction and yet based on my personal experience. So this begs the question, if the stories are based on my personal experience, then why are they fiction? Well, after much deliberation, that's the only way I could see to write them. I couldn't remember names and dates. I couldn't remember the details exactly. And in many instances, I had to create scenes and characters to make the stories work. To me, that's fiction.

In my previous two books, the writing was a lot easier. Each one came with a built-in compelling story line. Before I even started, I had a beginning, middle, and end. I had a complete story. For the most part, all I had to do was remember what happened and write it down. I always knew where the stories were heading. The compelling story line was already there.

This story is different.

My adventure to the Philippines back in 1989 didn't have a compelling story line. OK, maybe it did, but I couldn't find it. What it did have was a bunch of isolated stories. Stories I wanted to tell. Stories I felt were interesting. Stories I wanted to share with the world.

So, I began writing.

I'd write down one story, hit the save button, and start writing the next one. I kept writing. That is, until I ran out of stories. Then I became stuck. Stuck like a bug on a fly strip. Stuck like a saber-toothed tiger in a tar pit. Stuck like a Long Island Expressway rush-hour commuter. I wasn't moving. Without a compelling story line, I was dead in the water.

My individual stories—perhaps interesting on their own—were not really connected. The only thing tying them together was chronology. So, essentially, when I was done, I had a glorified travel log—"I did this, I went there, I met so-and-so, I danced, I sang, and then I went home." But I didn't want to write a travel log. I wanted to write a story—a heartfelt story. In order to do that, I needed a compelling story line. I didn't have one. I went searching.

And this represented new territory for me. How do you look for a story line ... a compelling one? I had no idea. (I still don't!) But after thinking about it for a while—a long while—I decided to research the Philippines, specifically Clark Air Base. I started reading personal accounts from people stationed there. It was from one of these accounts that I got the idea for the central caper in this book. It's something I never would have dreamed up—way too clever. The crime was pulled off in a mystifying way. They never caught the "geniuses" who did it. I decided this would be the crime for my story. I liked it because it's clever but also because it's based on something that really happened. So, when someone challenges, "That's impossible, couldn't happen," I can confidently say, "But it did." Does the phrase "Truth is stranger than fiction" mean anything to you?

Now that I had a caper, I went looking for a character—someone I could build the story around. My only criteria: it had to be a Filipino. I had several serious contenders, but I finally settled on a young boy I met briefly on the streets of Angeles city way back in late March 1989.

Once I had these two main ingredients—a caper and a character—I began rewriting the story, starting from the middle and working outward. This approach gave me targets, it gave me focus, and it allowed me to connect the stories, even if only loosely. Is that how you're supposed to write stories? Don't ask me. But that's how I went about fixing my "stuck" problem.

Now I was back to writing again. I had a destination. But I still had a lurking problem. I'd say my problem was similar to military-aircraft in-flight refueling—it's easy to understand the general concept, but it takes skill to do it. The devil is in the details. I wouldn't want somebody refueling my airplane who claims "I'm an expert!" because he or she read the manual once during a coffee break. It's one thing to say, "In-flight aircraft refueling is easy; just connect the hose, and start pumping jet fuel." It's another thing to be able to do it. It's called experience, skills, and know-how. And it involves lots of *details*!

Well, my lurking problem was how to connect my caper with my character. Yes, I had a general idea, but just like the coffee-break in-flight aircraft-refueling expert, I had no skills, no experience, and no know-how. I'd never done it before. Even so, I didn't let this obstacle stop me. I continued typing away, believing I would eventually figure it out. I confidently moved forward with the project, believing the answer would appear and my lurking problem would be solved.

And where did I get this belief?

Glad you asked.

For me, the most difficult part of making the connection between caper and character was this—you've got to be creative.

I have a challenge with creative. But luckily I could consult someone who's proven over the years to be very creative. A man named Stephen King. I consulted Mr. King via his book, *On Writing*. I'd read it once before, but when I became stuck with this story, I read it again. Because I was in desperate need of a story line, I got a lot more out of his book the second time through. I paid special attention to his advice on plot.

I was seeking a plot. I wanted something clever like an Agatha Christie who-done-it novel. But my attempts at "clever" kept turning into "corny." I started getting bogged down. I started fearing the keyboard. Like before, I felt dead in the water, not moving, going under—drowning.

But when I took Mr. King's advice on plot, life got better. I started to get my nose and mouth above water; I could breathe again. Finally, I swam to shore, dried off, and got back to the keyboard.

Mr. King's advice on plot is essentially this—*relax*! Don't get hung up on it. Let the story unfold on its own. According to Mr. King, the author's job is to uncover the story that's already there. Just keep writing, and let the story come out. Keep asking "What if?" questions, and let the characters act out their roles. I accepted his advice and began letting the characters take me where they wanted to go. I didn't fight it.

The story is written from the perspective of a young air-force second lieutenant named Sean Mitchell. This character is based on me. I like using Sean in my fiction stories because it makes the writing a lot easier. All I have to do is explain everything from my perspective. I don't have to be all-knowing. I just tell it how I see it.

This book involved some soul-searching. While I generally try to keep things light if I can, this story exposes a challenging issue. Why pick a challenging issue? After all, fiction means I can write about whatever I want. Why not pick something upbeat? Why not pick something easygoing?

Here's why. I boldly took Mr. King's advice: "Stories...pretty much make themselves. The job of the writer is to give them a place to grow. Stories are found things, like fossils in the ground. Stories are relics, part of an undiscovered preexisting world. The writer's job is...to get as much of each one out of the ground intact as possible."

So, that's what I did. I started hunting for the story. I went searching and digging like a treasure hunter, like an archaeologist.

The story you're about to read is what I found, what I dug up. Hopefully, I got most of it out of the ground intact.

Dave Ives
Alice Springs, Northern Territory, Australia
December 2016

1. DREAMS OF THE PHILIPPINES

How was your trip, Sean?" asked my coworker Ken. "I want to hear all about it. What an adventurer. Exotic trip to Hawaii...must be nice being a single guy. I could never go off on a trip like that; wife would never let me, although I'd love to. C'mon, tell me what happened. Give me all the mushy details!"

I sat there with my hands on the side of my head, looking down onto the big black and white government calendar on my desk. I remember staring at the month, April, and the year, 1989, in big bold font. My mind was ten thousand miles away.

His question knocked me back into the here and now. I pondered how to answer. "What do I say? I can't tell him what really happened. He'll never believe it. He'll think I've flipped. He'll say I'm making it all up."

It was seven in the morning, my first day back after being away on military leave. I took off for Hawaii with plans to spend two glorious weeks on the islands, relaxing and taking it easy. But that's not what happened. Instead, I ventured from the Aloha state to a place known as the Pearl of the Orient, an enchanted destination floating in the middle of the South China Sea—the Philippines.

As I sat at my desk, I did something a bit goofy. I didn't care if Ken was watching. I did it anyway. I reached over with my right hand and patted my left arm; I reached over with my left hand and patted my right arm, and then I patted my thighs. I wanted to make sure I wasn't dreaming, that I was really back home and still in one piece. I then returned to my original pose—hands on the side of my head, elbows on the desk, and head down looking at the calendar.

This mini-self-check reminded me of the time I fell asleep at the wheel driving across Nebraska. I was en route to my brother's wedding in South Dakota. The road was straight, flat, and deserted. The strong wind blew the fresh fallen snow from north to south as I travelled east in my 1985 Toyota Corolla. I intended to pull over and rest, but I kept telling myself, "One more mile."

I remember waking up to the sound of metal smacking metal. I opened my eyes just in time to see the reflector pole snap forward and then felt the car jolting up and down over the rough rocky gravel on the side of the road. I slammed the brakes so hard I could almost see my toes sticking out the front grille. Now I was awake. The car came to a rest. I shut off the engine. I sat there perfectly still listening to the silence. I took a few moments to orient myself. I wondered if I had died. I remember crossing my arms to grab myself. Then I reached down and grabbed my thighs. I wanted to verify I was alive. I wanted to make sure all my body parts were still intact. I wondered if it was just a bad dream.

If that roadside reflector pole had been a tree, I would have been dead.

I was lucky.

As I sat at my desk that morning, I had a similar feeling. My trip to the Philippines—did it really happen? Did I really go there and experience what my memory tells me? Or am I just dreaming? Am I just waking up from a dream and none of it really happened? Hey, maybe that's it; that would explain everything—it was just a dream, not real, didn't happen.

But just like my falling-asleep-at-the-wheel experience, my trip to the Philippines was real. It happened. I did it. And all the memories were still in my head. I didn't imagine them. They happened.

And these memories were turning into dreams. I would have dreams about my experience: some exciting, some depressing, some inspiring, some heartbreaking, some motivating, and some— like my Nebraska near-death experience—terrifying! The memories were still in my head. And they got there because it all happened. Now they were coming back to me as dreams—dreams of the Philippines.

I sat there wondering. "What do I tell Ken? How do I tell him what happened?"

We usually spent a few minutes each morning socializing. The work day didn't officially start until 7:30 a.m., so we'd take five minutes or so discussing the latest. The latest that morning was my Hawaii adventure.

My other coworker, Charlie, was listening; he wanted to know too. And my boss, Captain Jameson, stood at the cubical entrance, anxiously awaiting my response. Ken and Charlie were both air-force second lieutenants like me.

We worked in the engineering section at the Second Communications Squadron on Buckley Air National Guard Base just outside of Denver.

They were eager to hear my story.

I wanted to tell them. I wanted to blurt it all out. I needed to get it off my chest. But there was too much to tell. And as I thought about what happened, it sounded ridiculous; they'd never believe me. They'd laugh me out of the office, maybe even out of the air force. And I couldn't tell them everything anyway. I'd get in trouble. I'd have to leave parts out. I'd have to make parts up. I'd have to create a false narrative in order to preserve my air-force career.

Why?

'Cause it's crazy—other-world crazy. I could barely believe my story, and I'd lived through it. I knew it was real. I knew it happened. But that doesn't make it believable. Just because something is real doesn't mean you can get anyone to believe it. Hey, I've seen that before. You tell the truth, and they look at you like you're from an alien planet. "Yeah right; sure, we believe you. Anything you say, Sean."

I made a few attempts to retell the story in my mind to see if I could make it sound reasonable. No go. Every angle I tried sounded nuts. There's no way I could tell the story the way it happened and make it sound believable. In two minutes he'd be laughing me out of the office. "Great story, Sean. What an imagination! Ever consider a career as a fantasy writer?"

Finally, I let my arms drop to my desk. Then I looked over and said, "Ken, I don't want to talk about it. Not right now. I got a lot of work to catch up on; no time to chat. I'll tell you about it someday."

That was out of character for me. I was usually upbeat, excited, and talkative. I was showing a new side, a side of me that didn't exist before my trip. I had changed.

Capt. Jameson, Charlie, and Ken let out a collective sigh. Ken voiced his objection, "Give me a break! C'mon, you can't be serious! You're really not going to tell us what happened? You're kidding, right?"

I wasn't kidding. They dropped it. We never talked about it again.

But now I'm ready to tell the story. So, to my office mates back in Denver all those years ago—here's what happened.

2. HAWAII

He was sitting next to me. We were both perched on a low concrete wall surrounding a large indoor plant. It was just the two of us with our duffel bags.

I wanted to talk to him. He's the kind of guy who draws you in—a leader. I felt that if I talked to him, some of his leadership aura would rub off on me. So, I lobbed an easy serve over the conversational tennis net. "How's life in the army?"

He was decked out in full dress-blue army uniform. I glanced at his medals. I saw one with a rifle and another with a parachute. From this quick glance, I figured he was infantry and graduated from jump school at Fort Benning. He looked like he was heading off for a formal military function. But he wasn't. He was waiting for a plane just like me. We were both hanging out at the Hickam Air Force Base Military Airlift Command (MAC) terminal. I had time. I figured he had time—let's talk.

"Oh, it's fine, sir. I still get frustrated now and again, but overall, I like it." He answered in a sharp, forceful, yet polite manner.

I felt funny. I always did when I heard someone call me "sir." Especially when the other person is older and has more military experience. He looked and acted the part—a tough seasoned army soldier. I felt outclassed.

As I observed this model soldier, I thought about my twin brother. He used to make fun of me because I joined the air force. He did it in humorous fashion. "Hey, Sean, did you hear about the guy who couldn't get in the military so he joined the air force?" Well, these words seemed appropriate as I sat next to a real live ground pounder, an infantryman, a soldier trained for combat.

But I was a second lieutenant, and he was a sergeant. He's enlisted; I'm an officer. He called me "sir." And that's how enlisted are supposed to address officers, so he did. He's a pro.

I wanted to know more. He mentioned the word "frustrated." I continued, "So, what are the things that frustrate you?"

I wasn't quite ready for his passionate response. But I asked and now—ready or not—I was going to get it.

"First, I've been in the army for thirteen years, and I'm sick and tired of training my officers. Every time we get a new lieutenant, I have to train him. I've never had one who knew what he was doing. I don't understand why I have to train a guy who's supposed to be my boss, supposed to be my leader. They don't know a thing, especially when it comes to the field. I have to show them everything—from setting up the tents to getting the 'water buffalo' situated. Sometimes I just tell them to go get coffee, and I organize everything—just relax. I'll set up camp. Then, just when I have an officer half trained up, he leaves for a desk assignment at headquarters.

"I'd say that's my biggest frustration. Getting officers who have no idea what they're doing. How can they possibly lead troops when they're incompetent? How can they expect us to respect officers when they don't have a clue, got no idea what they're doing? Seems like most of them are just trying to get promoted, gaming the system; they don't care about the army. The troops see right through this, and it destroys morale."

I took a deep breath. He let me have it. I asked for it. I got it. I didn't mind. I kind of liked it. I liked hearing his straight talk. Beats the heck out of some politically corrected canned response that has no emotion, no feeling, and no value. His response had value. I could feel his frustration. He said he was frustrated, and now I knew why. I decided to change direction, so I hit the conversation ball to the other side of the court.

"What do you like about the army?"

As I listened to his response, I respected him even more.

"I like the comradery. I like the friends I've made, the great people I've met, the incredible adventures I've been through. Have you ever seen an army on the move? Do you know what it's like to see a division loaded up for battle and taking up the whole countryside? Tank tracks tearing up the earth, convoy trucks lined up so far they disappear past the horizon? It's awesome. It's like nothing you'll ever see or experience as a civilian. I love it. I love being in the army and being a soldier."

I thought, "Wow! We need soldiers like this in the army." They say the noncommissioned officers (NCOs) are the backbone of the military. I agree. Without backbones like him, the military would be nothing but a big ball of jelly, a mush, a big expensive scrap heap with no form. The dedicated NCOs keep it all together, keep it running, and keep it alive.

I wanted to salute him. I resisted and followed up with more questioning.

"So, where are you off to, Sergeant Morales?" I noted his big army name badge with his last name appearing like a miniature billboard.

"I'm heading home to the Philippines. I was born there. I grew up there, going to see my family. I haven't seen them for almost a year, so I'm taking a military flight back home. It's a pain having to fly military because you can get stuck on the waiting list. But the price is right—free. And I'm the only one traveling, so it should be easy getting a seat. My wife and kids are living back in the Philippines, so I'm taking advantage of the free flights to see them."

No surprise there. I was waiting for the plane heading off to the Philippines too. I wasn't going there to see my family. I was just going there. I'd taken two weeks leave from my air-force desk job in Colorado and found myself in Hawaii. I'd flown commercial all the way.

I'd planned to spend two weeks in Hawaii, but I couldn't find a place to stay on base. Well, I could, but it was awkward. The billeting (hotel) on Hickam is always in high demand. That's what I discovered—everyone wants to go to Hawaii. My first two nights, I was lucky enough to get a room, but I'd have to check out each day and reapply. It was a hassle. I decided to leave.

While waiting to get a room each day, I got talking to some of the old timers—retired military—and they encouraged me to check out the MAC flights. "They got flights going to Clark all the time, and it's a lot cheaper in the Philippines than here in Hawaii. You'll have a great time, and it won't cost you nearly as much. Why don't you look into it?"

So, I did.

And that's how I ended up at the Hickam terminal waiting to catch one of the many flights heading to Clark Air Base.

I wasn't used to seeing enlisted army-rank insignia. I knew the air-force enlisted rank insignia like the back of my hand. I'd been enlisted air force for almost six years before getting my commission, so the rank was second nature. Also, I was fairly familiar with navy enlisted rank because we worked alongside navy personnel back in Colorado, where I was stationed. But I hardly ever bumped into soldiers, so I wasn't quite sure of the army rank. I figured this was a chance to test my knowledge.

"I see you've got three chevrons and one rocker arm—that's a staff sergeant right?"

"Yes, sir; you got it."

Staff Sergeant (SSgt) Morales and I were both stuck waiting until we could catch the next flight out to the Philippines. He had a higher priority than I had. He was on morale leave, so he got first dibs on available seats. I was just on ordinary leave, so I was near the bottom of the priority list. But when I looked up at the huge schedule board, there were flights heading for Clark Air Base all the time. Looked like a done deal. I was confident I could hitch a ride. And I was confident there must be huge numbers of flights coming back from the Philippines, so I wasn't worried about getting home either.

The announcement rang out over the loudspeaker, "All passengers proceed to the counter for passenger call out. We'll be booking by priority. If your name is called, proceed to the tarmac and board."

SSgt Morales got called first. He bid me farewell, "See you, sir. Nice talking to you. Enjoy your trip to the Philippines."

"Nice talking to you too, Sergeant Morales; enjoy your visit with your family."

After watching so many people board the plane, I figured it was full and I'd have to take another one. The young airman calling out the names shifted to the right—facing away from me—and I could barely hear his words. But it sounded like my name. I called out, "Did you say Lieutenant Mitchell?"

He responded angrily, as if I just stepped on his brown paper bag lunch. "I did. And I told everyone to listen up—were you listening? I told you during my initial briefing, if I call your name and you don't respond, I go to the next name. Lieutenant, you almost got crossed off my list. OK, you can board."

And that's what I call military customer service.

I *was* listening. Everyone in that crowd was listening with great intensity. We were all focused on getting a seat on the plane. But it's difficult to hear when the announcer looks the other way and mumbles. I just guessed he called my name. I wasn't sure. But I'm glad I asked the question, or he would have kept reading off the names, and I would have missed the flight.

This is a typical case of "who's got the power." The airman had it; I didn't. He was in charge of this operation, and I was just another "military" customer. A military customer is nothing like a customer. A military customer is at the mercy of the person behind the desk. I would imagine this is the way it is in a socialist state—a communist state. People wait in line for the privilege of being served by the folks in power. I'd had enough glimpses of this in the military to know I want no part of it.

This "who's got the power" gig works both ways. If you are friends with the person in power, you can jump the line. It's worked for me on occasion during my military career. It can also work against you if the person in charge doesn't owe you any favors or chooses to arbitrarily exercise power or—God forbid—doesn't like you.

I'll share a couple of examples where this "who's got the power" syndrome worked in my favor.

First, I remember calling over to Lowry Air Force Base to make a dental appointment. The guy on the other end of the line says, "You got the wrong number; you need to call the appointment desk. But before you do, I'm wondering, were you stationed at Mather Air Force Base?"

"Yes," I replied. "Why do you ask?"

"Did your roommate work in the Flight Surgeon's Office?"

"How did you know?"

"Are you Sean Mitchell?"

"Yeah."

"I used to work next door to your roommate Leonel from Portugal. I'm George Campbell. I used to live in the hospital barracks with you."

"Oh yeah, I thought your voice sounded familiar. How are you?"

"I'm doing great. Love it here at Lowry. Congratulations on becoming an officer."

"Thanks."

"Look, Lieutenant Mitchell, normally you have to make an appointment at the front desk, but I think they're backed up for the next two months. Just tell me what's a good day for you, and I'll book it right now.

"Oh, and by the way, do you remember Airman Wilkins? She used to live in the dormitory with us—dental tech."

"'Course I do. Melanie. We got along well."

"Well, she's stationed here now. And she's a staff sergeant. I'll book you in with her. Let's see. She's got an opening this Wednesday morning; you want it?

Now that's service.

Another time I got a ticket for speeding on Lowry Air Force Base. The military-security policeman seemed to enjoy pulling over an officer. I think he got me for doing a couple of miles an hour over the speed limit, doing twenty-two in a twenty zone or something like that. Didn't matter. I wasn't getting off. He didn't know me, and he didn't owe me any favors. He did the right thing. He did his job. He issued me a speeding ticket. I didn't like it. I was hoping he'd let me off with a warning. He didn't. Too bad...for me.

But luckily I did know someone at the security-police office.

The next morning the phone rang at my desk. I'd just arrived in my office at Buckley Air National Guard Base where I worked as a satellite-systems engineer. It was my friend Alley calling over from the security-police office at Lowry. I knew Alley from the Catholic Church on base. She and I were members of the "young adults" group made up of mostly single military folks. There were only two officers in the group, me and a young military doctor who worked in the base clinic. Alley was an airman first class.

"Did you get a ticket on base last night?" Alley asked with a lighthearted inflection in her voice.

"Yeah, how did you know?"

"I saw it sitting in my in-basket this morning. Did you tell your commander yet?"

"No, I haven't had a chance."

"Good. Don't do it. I tore up the ticket. You can throw away your copy."

Alley started laughing. She thought it was funny. I thought she'd just demonstrated awesome power—the power to rip up on-base traffic tickets.

Again, this was a case where "who's got the power" worked in my favor.

But it can also backfire and work against you. The person in power can make your life miserable.

I'll share one glaring example I heard first hand from the person in power, the person doling out the misery.

"I make the decisions in my work center. I save the air force lots of money," explained my lady airman friend who worked in the Travel Management Office (TMO). I was off duty at some gathering, mulling around, drinking coffee.

"How do you figure?" I asked wanting her to explain what she meant.

"Just the other day an airman came in with just his duffel bag. That's all the belongings he had. He wanted to ship the duffel bag. I told him no. You have to carry it on the plane."

I couldn't understand where she was going with this, so I questioned further, "Is he authorized to ship his duffel bag?"

"'Course he is, but I'm not going to let him do that. I'm not going to waste air-force money because this airman is too lazy to carry his duffel bag! No way! He doesn't know the regulations; I do. I know he's authorized, but I don't want to waste government money shipping one lousy duffel bag! Forget it!"

I couldn't believe what I was hearing. A young airman simply wants to ship his duffel bag and she shuts him down to save the air-force money. So, let me get this straight: if the kid had a whole container full of junk, it would have been OK to ship it—air force will pay for that. But since he only came in with a fully stuffed duffel bag, it's too much of a burden to ship it? How do you figure?

She had the power. She exercised it. The young airman lugged his overstuffed duffel bag across the globe to further the cause of this power-hungry gal who wanted to save the air force a few bucks. She lost me on the logic. But she did make her message clear—she was in charge, she had the power, and she was prepared to use it.

The airman in the Hickam terminal had the power. He was in charge, and he was the one who decided if you rode on the airplane or not.

I've discovered the military is all about power. Not rank—power. If you've got the power, you get the prize.

And one of the biggest power levers is regulations. An airman who knows and follows the regulations can virtually rule like a king in his or her area of responsibility. If he wants something to happen—do a favor—he can make it happen by following the regulations. On the other hand, if he wants to stop something from happening—

crush someone of any rank—he can make it happen by following the regulations.

And I was reminded of this as the airman in charge of the terminal scolded me in front of the anxious crowd clamoring to get a seat on the transport plane to the Philippines. I realized he had the power to stop me from getting on the plane. He could have read the next name on the list just to show me he's the boss, to teach me a lesson. He didn't. But he did feel the need to show off a bit of power by giving me a public scolding—"Hey, look, y'all, I'm telling off the lieutenant!" I exercised my option to ignore him. Instead of respectfully listening to his diatribe, I walked straight past him as if he didn't exist. I ignored him like I would a barking dog.

* * *

The C-141 is a big airplane. It's designed to haul cargo. The big area in the back of the plane is a perfect platform for transporting everything from toothbrushes to tanks. It's also very handy for hauling a special category of cargo—humans.

It was my first time on-board a C-141 Starlifter. I looked around at the Spartan surroundings. There were pallets of cargo stacked toward the back and on the left side of the aircraft. On the right side was a hard bench with fishnet wall-hanging straps. Then to the front was a single row of proper airline seats. The seats looked ordinary, old, and used, as if they were hand-me-downs picked up at a secondhand store.

Then I noticed something—something missing. I searched for them. I saw none. Those of us in the back would be "flying blind."

Dave Ives

The C-141 design calls for a special feature—no windows in the cargo bay.

I took my place on the hard side bench, and the plane took off. Our first stop would be Andersen Air Force Base on the island of Guam. From there we'd take off for Clark Air Base, near Angeles City, Pampanga Province on the Island of Luzon, Philippines.

My most vivid memory of this flight is the cold and the noise. The C-141 is not a commercial aircraft and therefore not designed for passenger comfort. Passengers are just another category of cargo. We had the same comfort, luxury, and convenience as the crates stacked on the pallets.

3. GUAM

I entered the bus expecting some relief from the outside heat. No luck. I went from the blast oven flight line to the steam bath radiating greenhouse inside the bus. I was expecting the weather to be the same as Hawaii—perfect. No way. Guam was hot—damn hot. And damn humid too!

I looked for a seat. The choice was easy. There was only one left. As I approached the vacant seat, I noticed her, hunched over and rocking slightly. She glanced up at me with a look that said, "I'm in pain." I scanned the bus one more time looking for another option. I didn't want to sit with her. But my scanning only verified what I already knew—there were no other options. I sat down next to her.

"Hello!" I greeted my new neighbor with a spring in my voice hoping to lighten up the depressed atmosphere.

It didn't work. She started talking, telling her story like I was Doctor Phil, like she was on the Oprah show. I wasn't ready for it. I didn't want to hear it. I wanted something upbeat. Instead I got beaten down.

"My mother died. I'm going back to the Philippines for the funeral. I haven't seen her for two years. I was planning to go back last year, but I got too busy and put it off. Now she's dead. And I didn't get a chance to talk to her, no chance to say "good-bye." Now she's gone. Why didn't I go back last year? Why did I wait?"

I put away my fake smile and looked straight ahead through the big front window. I pretended to be searching for our aircraft, helping the driver locate the correct plane. I felt uncomfortable with the lady's confession. I wanted the bus ride to be a short one. I didn't want this lady's depressed mood to rub off on me—too late! My lady friend and I sat silently as the bus drove across the blistering hot tarmac over to our waiting aircraft.

* * *

Somehow I managed to get one of the comfortable seats on the C-141. A blond-haired lady sat to my left. We hit it off immediately.

"Are you stationed at Clark?" she asked.

Just by looking at my uniform, she already knew three things about me. First, she knew I was in the air force. Next, she knew I was a second lieutenant. Third, she knew my last name—one peek at my name tag gave it away. Her question was appropriate. The plane was headed for Clark Air Force Base. It made sense that I was probably stationed there.

She was a good looking gal. Her long hair flopped back and forth as she accented her speech with appropriate head and hand movements. She was fun to be around.

"No, I'm just on leave from my duty station in Colorado. I was stuck in Hawaii and decided to catch a MAC flight to Clark, do some exploring. Why not? Figure I might as well take advantage of these free military flights."

The flights weren't really free, but they were so close it wasn't worth making the distinction. They charged me ten bucks. That was the price for folks on ordinary leave. If you were on morale leave, it was free.

She started filling me in on her story.

"I'm flying on to Cubi Point. My husband is a lieutenant commander, we're stationed at Subic."

"Cubi Point—where's that?" I asked.

"That's the airfield right next to Subic. They got flights going in and out of there all the time. You ought to come out for a visit. It's easy to catch a flight to Cubi. Just let me know when you get in, and I'll pick you up. Come on over the house for dinner."

I was taken aback by her quick invitation to visit as if we were long lost cousins. But I liked it. There seemed to be an immediate bond. In my time in the military, I experienced this bonding on occasion. It's strange, as if we're family. If you're in the military, you're family. No need for long introductions. No need for background checks. I trust you.

"I've only got about two weeks; then I got to be back at work. I don't know if I'll have time to duck out to Subic. But if I do, I'll let you know. Thanks for the invite; I appreciate it."

We continued our conversation. We laughed. We joked. We were like a couple of school kids wrapped up in our own little world, oblivious to anyone around us, carrying on like life is just a big happy adventure—not a worry in the world.

After our long gab session, we both fell asleep.

When I woke up, I did a little, "Where am I?" number and then oriented myself back to reality. "Let's see. I'm riding onboard a military cargo plane, facing backward in a relatively comfortable slightly reclined seat, on my way to Clark Air Base, and one other thing—my pretty lady friend is sound asleep, resting her head gently on my left shoulder." I gazed around the plane at the other passengers and saw the look in their eyes. If their eyes could speak, they would have said, "You two are married. She's your wife."

I didn't mind. Not one bit. I felt very comfortable having my lady friend use my left shoulder as a pillow. And I really didn't care what anyone thought. At that moment, I was enjoying life.

My blonde haired lady friend finally woke up. She lifted her head gently and smiled as if to say, "Thank you for the use of your comfortable shoulder." I smiled back. We both sat quietly facing straight ahead enjoying the loud roar of the aircraft engines.

* * *

My attention kept getting drawn to her. She was sitting on the hard metal bench on the right side of the aircraft. She was shivering. She was hunched over. It was the depressed lady from the bus. I felt sorry for her. I couldn't stand looking at her freezing.

I waved my arms to signal one of the medevac nurses and then asked her, "Have you got an extra blanket?"

"What?" She replied. The cabin engine noise drowned out my request.

I asked again except this time in a much higher volume and with associated hand gestures.

She seemed irritated by my request. As if blankets were reserved for patients, and I was a sissy for asking. She walked quickly to where the blankets were hidden, grabbed one, and then approached me. She stopped about three feet away and then threw the blanket at me as if to say, "Hey, I'm not your maid" or "I don't work for you." Then she looked away and went back to her seat and her crossword puzzle. Apparently, my request interrupted her concentration.

I got up from my comfortable seat and took the blanket over to the lady I met on the bus. I sat down and tapped her on the shoulder. She looked up, and I held out the blanket. She stared at me for a moment. I thought about wrapping the blanket around her but decided that might be a bit too forward and might frighten her. She appeared to be in a very delicate state of mind.

She turned slightly toward me, gently took the blanket, and began wrapping it around herself. When she finally got it adjusted the way she wanted, she looked up at me and said, "Thank you." I didn't hear the words but I could easily make them out by reading her lips. I replied in a low tone—even though I knew she couldn't hear me either over the aircraft noise—"You're welcome." She gave me a knowing look telling me she read my lips and understood. She then tucked her head into her knees under the blanket and retreated from our lip-reading conversation.

I sat there staring across the hull of the aircraft. I thought about what I could do to ease this lady's distress. I wanted to say something but everything that came to mind sounded corny. "Do you fly on military aircraft often? How are you enjoying the flight so far?" Nonsense—I kept thinking.

After a few minutes of focusing on the situation, an idea flashed before me. I thought back to a few days ago and a funeral I attended. A young girl—only eight years or so—was killed in a car accident. She was the daughter of a Sergeant who worked in our squadron. The mom survived the crash—very sad. The mom also happened to be from the Philippines. I remembered sitting in the church on Lowry Air Force Base thinking, "How do you cope with such a tragedy? This is when you need spiritual toughness. You need spiritual strength. Otherwise how do you carry on?"

I thought about the program from the funeral. It contained the twenty-third Psalm. I reached down into my right pocket and felt the folded paper. I'd worn the same military trousers to the funeral. The program was in my pocket. I pulled it out and then folded the paper showing only the page with the twenty-third Psalm. I sat there conducting an internal debate on whether or not to hand it to the lady. "What if she rejects it? What is she throws it on the floor? What if she's insulted? What if she gets upset? Is it appropriate for me to interfere? Should I just let her mourn her mother in her own way? Who am I to step in and think I can offer any help, offer anything, to ease her mental anguish?"

Then I thought about the positives. Whoever put this program together must have thought it would help the grieving parents get through the devastation of losing their daughter. Maybe there's healing power in the twenty-third Psalm. Maybe it can bring some relief. Maybe it can help.

I made my decision. I tapped her on the shoulder, and she popped her head out from under the blanket. I smiled and handed her the program opened up to the twenty-third Psalm. She took it from me and started reading.

I sat there worrying my action may have been the wrong thing to do. The doubt kicked back in, "Hey, what'd you do that for? What makes you think it's your job to try and cheer her up? You're going to look foolish. Why did you do that?"

In the middle of beating myself up, she looked over and did something that made me glad—glad I made a daring attempt to offer condolence. She smiled.

She followed up her smile with another surprise—she started a conversation. I struggled to hear her soft voice over the plane noise, but I somehow managed to capture every word.

"Where are you stationed?" she asked like an air-force newspaper reporter. Her expression and tone were upbeat and energetic. I was stunned at the transformation. I went with it.

"I'm stationed at Buckley Air National Guard Base in Colorado, just outside of Denver."

"How come you're going out to the Philippines?" she continued her line of questioning.

"I've got a few weeks off work and thought I'd catch a flight. Never been there before; thought it might be adventurous."

I stopped and waited for her to ask another question. She paused and looked deep into my eyes. Then she stated, "Thank you for giving me the twenty-third Psalm. After reading it I'm filled with strength. I realize I was just feeling sorry for myself. I was condemning myself for not seeing my mother before she died. I can't change that now. What's done is done. What I need to do is be strong. I need to be strong for my family back in the Philippines. I need to go home and offer healing to my family. I need to offer hope and give thanks that my mother was such a good mother. She raised nine children who loved her very much, who respected her. I'm going home to celebrate the great life of my mother. I'm going home to spend time with my family and friends and remember the great moments we had with my mother. Yes, thank you so much for letting me read the twenty-third Psalm. I'm so glad."

"What's your name?"

"I'm Sean"

"Hi, Sean, I'm Peaches."

Yes, her name was Peaches. I ain't making this stuff up. I could never come up with a name that corny. When she told me, I swear my head involuntarily shot back an inch or so—recoiling from the ridiculousness. "Peaches? Did she say 'Peaches'?"

How did she get the name Peaches? She didn't look anything like a peach. She had black hair, brown skin, and brown eyes. She looked like the poster child for a Jenny Craig diet advertisement, no fat on her anywhere. Her silky smooth skin showed no sign of peach fuzz.

She seemed very proud of her name—very happy to call herself Peaches. And if she was OK with it, so was I.

"Glad to meet you, Peaches." I tested out saying her name; see if maybe by saying it, it won't sound so corny. I didn't feel like asking her how she got that name. I figured it was best to let her ask the questions during this delicate time.

She continued telling me about herself, "My husband and three children are back in Guam. They wanted to come along, but he couldn't get off work, and the kids are in school. It was just too tough, so it's only me on the trip. But I had to go. I knew I had to go home. I couldn't live with myself if I didn't go."

Eventually, the conversation stopped. The aircraft noise won out. Looking content, cozy, and comfortable under her blanket, Peaches drifted off to sleep.

* * *

I looked to my left, past sleeping Peaches, and noticed one of the flight crew drawing on a pad of notepaper. I watched as his left hand held a pencil and scraped across the paper, leaving incredibly skillful drawings in its wake. I was fascinated by his talent.

I pulled my eyes back to get a wider angle on the scene. I now focused on the crew member instead of zeroing in only on the drawing. He looked familiar. I'd seen him before somewhere, but where? I racked my brains.

My curiosity took over, so I decided my first step would be to sit next to him and ask about his drawing. Chances are I don't know him, but it would be an easy way for me to make sure. I felt I knew him from somewhere.

"Hey, that's some impressive drawing you're doing there," I stated in as homey a way possible for a boy from New England.

"Yeah, it's my hobby," he replied, still looking down at his drawing. "Been doing it for years; it's a way for me to relax, especially on these long medevac missions."

His voice sounded familiar.

He looked cool in his flight suit. We used to call them "bags" back at Mather Air Force Base near Sacramento, California, where I was stationed as a medic. Mather was a SAC (Strategic Air Command) base. As such, we'd see B-52 and KC-135 pilots and aircrew all the time wearing their uniform of choice—the bag. The ladies loved it. They used to flock to the pilots, navigators, flight engineers, or any man who looked like a pilot—any man wearing a bag.

My drawing buddy happened to be a buck sergeant. They've done away with that rank now, but it's the same as a senior airman— three stripes, E-4 rank. The only difference is the star—buck-sergeant star is solid blue; senior-airman star is not colored in. I made it to senior airman during my time as a medic but never made it to buck sergeant.

He had dirty blond hair—a bit messy from wearing his flight cap. I could see his side profile—square jaw line, skinny lips, and short nose. He reminded me of my best buddy from tech school. But that was seven years earlier. What are the chances—not very good?

He kept drawing, and I kept asking questions. "Where are you stationed?"

"Clark. We're on our way back from a mission. Dropped some patients off at Travis, and now we're on the return flight. I do some of my best drawings on these long flights. Be way too boring if I didn't have my pencil and pad."

Travis Air Force Base is in northern California, about half way between Sacramento and San Francisco. I'd been there a few times on ambulance runs, dropping off patients at the hospital.

My curiosity was piqued. This guy sounded just like my best friend from tech school. And my best friend was a lefty too, and he liked to draw. Could it be him? I still wasn't sure. I still wasn't convinced.

I must have piqued his curiosity too because he suddenly looked up at me. Our faces met. I stared at him for only a second or so, but that was enough time for me to perform a complete study of his features to verify what was now obvious.

I spoke first—only one word, "Jim?"

Now it was his turn—one word, "Sean?"

We both started laughing so loud we drowned out the C-141 engine noise!

"What are you doing here?" shouted Jim.

"I'm on leave. I'm visiting Clark, check out the Philippines, a bit of adventure."

"How long is your leave?"

"I've got about two weeks, but I've got to leave time to catch a flight back to Hawaii, where I pick up my commercial flight back to Denver."

"Great! I'll show you around. The first thing we do after a mission is get a back rub downtown. It's the best. You'll love it, so relaxing.

"Congratulations on becoming a lieutenant. How did you manage that?"

"Well, the air force sent me to Ohio State to get my engineering degree; then I went to OTS (Officer Training School), and now I'm here." I explained in short fashion.

"What are you doing now—what's your job?"

"Satellite-systems engineer, working on Buckley Air National Guard Base near Denver. It's a far cry from my days as a medic. Hey, you got a pretty cool job on the medevac team; how did you pull that one off?"

"I put in for it and got accepted. Way better than working in the hospital. We get flight pay and everything. I love it."

It was great to see Jim again. He was my best buddy from tech school back in late 1981 and early 1982 on Sheppard Air Force Base. I enjoyed tech school. I made good friends there. It was exciting.

'Course, anything would be exciting after getting out of basic training. I think that's what made tech school so enjoyable—the contrast to basic training. Tech school felt like freedom compared to basic. At tech school we could do things like ... go off base! Crazy stuff like ... watch TV on our off-duty time. I used to cherish Sunday afternoons at the base recreation center watching Clint Eastwood Rawhide reruns.

One of my fondest memories of tech school is the chow hall. I remember how I enjoyed the food and best of all, the serving ladies. The whole experience was uplifting. Maybe it was just the contrast to basic training where everyone seemed to treat us as fixtures to be bossed around, utensils to be used—junk. But at tech school, I remember walking through the chow-hall line and being greeted by the serving lady, "Help ya, Airman! What you havin'? We got eggs, fried, scrambled, or how 'bout some good ole SOS? Let me know, sunshine."

I almost fell over. I wanted to jump over the counter and hug the middle-aged lady who seemed to take on the role of my mother. I got this same friendly treatment from all the serving ladies. They sort of looked the same to me—a bit overweight, middle aged, and big smiling faces.

One day I got a very pleasant surprise. I was moving through the chow line, scanning for choices, and heard, "Airman Mitchell, you hungry? You always hungry; what's you having this fine morning?"

I looked up at my cheery serving lady, and then my brain scrambled as I gazed upon something stunning—the beautiful young lady standing next to her. Even in her serving-lady outfit, she looked gorgeous. Now, maybe this was because I'd been cooped up too long in the military setting, but maybe not. Maybe she was just plain "North Texas gorgeous," and I was witnessing God's good work. I would soon discover something delightful—Wichita Falls produces some amazingly beautiful ladies.

Again, I wanted to jump over the counter and hug the middle-aged serving lady as she introduced me, "Airman Mitchell, I want you to meet my daughter."

I tried to steady my flapping jaw as I searched for something clever to say. My random-thought-generator kicked in, and I just grabbed the first word that popped out.

"Hi."

The serving lady's daughter smiled, and I collapsed—mentally. Her smile drove her beauty factor off the scales. I was in love.

I bumped and banged up against the metal serving tray rack as I rubber-legged my way to the cash register. What a great feeling. It was embarrassing, but I enjoyed the moment anyway. I enjoyed gazing upon such a beautiful lady. It was pure unadulterated pleasure.

As you can tell, after basic training, it didn't take much to make me happy—to entertain me!

Yeah, I enjoyed my time at tech school, and Jim was a big part of it. We hung out together, studied together, and played a lot of pinball during classroom breaks. I wasn't a big pinball fan, but Jim was. If I wanted to hang out with him, I had to hang out at the pinball machines. I really got to know Jim as he'd play pinball and then tell me stories from his past.

"Ever been in jail, Mitch?"

"No."

"I have. I broke a pool queue across a guy's head. We were playing pool. I won. He wouldn't pay. He threatened me—him and all his buddies at the bar. I cracked him across the head, and the other guys scattered. I got a month in jail for that one. Judge agreed it was self-defense but still had to give me some punishment."

I found Jim's story hard to believe. It seemed out of character. He was a good troop. He didn't get into trouble. Apparently, before he joined the air force, Jim hung out with a rough crowd. He had to defend himself. So he did.

Jim continued, "I was glad the air force let me join. 'Course I couldn't get into a lot of jobs. Any job requiring a security clearance was out. But luckily the medical field was wide open. They needed medics. I was OK with that. Glad I got in."

On the other hand, I became a medic because I joined the service without a guaranteed job. I went in "open-general." That meant the air force could do what they wanted with me. I chose open-general because it allowed me to get in the quickest. If I wanted a guaranteed job, I'd have to wait up to a year to get in. I wanted no part of that. I wanted in now. Therefore, I agreed to go in the open-general category. The air force needed medics, so that's where I went. And that's how I ended up in tech school with my good buddy Jim.

And now I was reunited with Jim on a noisy C-141 headed for Clark Air Base in the Philippines.

4. CLARK AIR BASE

I closed my eyes as I waited anxiously for the wheels to touch the runway. I was excited about the prospect of visiting the Philippines. I'd heard about it. I'd listened to the stories from the troops stationed there. I'd read books about it. I read the boring encyclopedia articles about it. Even the boring entries sounded exciting.

The Philippines - made up of over seven thousand islands. What's the exact number? Who knows? A Filipina beauty pageant contestant explained it best. One of the judges asked, "How many islands are there in the Philippines?" Her reply drew great laughter, applause, and admiration, "Do you mean high tide or low tide?"

The Philippines - under Spanish rule for over three hundred years. Manila was the oriental hub for the Spanish galleon trade. European goods came in; Filipino and Chinese goods went out. Along with the exchange of goods came the exchange of ideas, the collision of cultures—East and West—creating a flavorful mix of Malay and Madrid.

The Philippines - a US colony for forty-eight years. The Americans took the islands in 1898 after a short war with Spain. The Filipinos weren't consulted. The United States granted independence on the

Fourth of July, 1946, but the American influence continued. Now the islands were home for two massive US military installations—Clark Air Base and Subic Bay Naval Base. Hotdogs, apple pie, and baseball were now thrown into the cultural mix.

I felt the bump; I heard the noise. The wheels made contact with the runway. The plane touched down. We landed. My heart jumped a bit as I imagined what I'd see when the door opened up. I would gaze upon—for the first time—Clark Air Base, near Angeles City, Pampanga, island of Luzon, Philippines.

I was somewhat disappointed to discover the tarmac and terminal at Clark looked much like any other air-force base. Nothing really to tell me I was in an exotic far eastern location. It didn't take long, and I didn't have to go far to realize I wasn't in Kansas anymore. But my first glimpse of Clark looked pretty ordinary—just another air-force flight line.

* * *

"OK, I'll pick you up at the officers' quarters. I'll be there in about an hour, and then we're off to get back rubs. You're gonna love it." Jim reminded me of our plans as we walked across the terminal.

He was off to the barracks, and I was off to locate a room for the night. I'd start at the visiting officers' quarters and try my luck there.

As I headed for the exit, I heard her voice, "Sean, hope you have a nice visit to the Philippines. Stay safe; be careful."

I looked to my right and saw Peaches. Her big smiling face was miles away from the depressed slumping blob I witnessed on the bus in Guam. "I'll be fine. You take care as well."

I thought our conversation was over, but she started walking quickly over to me. I stood there waiting to see what was going to happen next. She put down her bags, opened her arms wide, and threw them around me.

"Thank you. Thank you for cheering me up on the flight. I was a wreck, but your note made all the difference. I can face my family now. I'm going to be strong. I'm going to help them instead of being a burden."

As quickly as she came toward me, she went away. I watched as she picked up her bags and disappeared into the crowd of people leaving the terminal.

I felt good. I was enjoying my first few moments in the Philippines.

* * *

I walked into the expansive ornate lobby. "Wow!" I whispered to myself. "I get to stay here? This is great."

I caught a base cab from the terminal over to the visiting officers' quarters, a building called Chambers Hall. I was pleasantly surprised when the cabbie accepted my US dollars. I think he charged me two bucks. I had to make sure I kept plenty of one-dollar bills on hand to pay for my transport around base. During this one taxi drive, I learned something very important about Clark

Air Base—it's huge! Walking was out of the question. If I wanted to get around in a reasonable timeframe, I had to use the ever present, efficient, and inexpensive base taxi system.

I noticed the lady behind the counter and the lobby had something in common—they were both glamorous. They were a nice match. The opulent setting made me think of *Star Trek*—"Did Scotty just beam me over to some luxurious Monte Carlo five-star resort?" I felt out of place. "What's an ordinary guy like me doing in a swanky place like this?"

I approached the beautiful lady and almost blurted out, "Will you marry me?" Instead, I caught myself, regained my composure and asked, "Hello, I'm wondering if you have any rooms available?"

Then she did something I would have to get used to during my visit to the Philippines—something I wasn't used to, something I really enjoyed, something that melted my heart—she smiled.

"Yes, sir, we have one room left. But it's only for one night. We're running standby because we have a lot of flight crews here from Okinawa on a big training exercise. They have first priority. So, you need to check out tomorrow morning and then come back in the afternoon to see if we have a room. OK, sir?"

I enjoyed watching her talk. She glided. She spoke with ease. She spoke as if I were an important person. She showed respect to a lowly second lieutenant, a guy desperately looking for a place to store his gear and get cleaned up.

Her deal sounded a lot like my goofy situation back in Hawaii but it also sounded great. I get a room now. Tomorrow I'll have to hunt again, but for now, I get a room. "I'll take it."

I threw my bag on the bed and looked out the window. What a setup! Again, I felt out of place—way too nice. I was used to ordinary accommodation. This place was top of the line: royal bed spread, fancy curtains, plush carpet, and a private bathroom. I thought I was in the VIP suite. But I was assured it was just an ordinary VOQ (visiting officers' quarters) room, nothing special, and they're all the same.

I cleaned up a bit, got into some comfortable cool attire and ran down to the hotel lobby with the excitement of a kid on Christmas morning. I waited anxiously for Jim to pick me up.

"Hop in, Sean!" Jim yelled from the car. I double-timed it from the front door of Chambers Hall into the rust laden jalopy. I squeezed into the back seat and shut the door half expecting it to fall off.

"Sean, these are my friends from the dorm." Jim rattled off the names. The car was packed, three in the front seat, four in the back. "After every mission we visit the ladies for a back rub. Never miss it. Only two bucks—can you swing two bucks, Sean?"

I was pumped. Here I am, on the ground in the Philippines for only an hour or so, and I'm off to get a back rub—for only two bucks— with my old tech school buddy and a car load of his friends from the barracks.

The car was a junk box, but I wasn't complaining. It beat the heck out of walking and the price was right—free. But it was certainly a worry. It made loud death-bed sounding engine noises, like a coughing B-17 aircraft ready to explode. It looked like it needed a new coat of rust—the old one was on its last legs. The car had the driving characteristics of horse-drawn buggy. Every bump in the road became a painful jolt shooting up my spinal column. I figured the suspension was made of the same material as the body—rust.

I looked around at my fellow passengers, and they all seemed quite content with this fine piece of machinery. Cigarettes lit, smoke blowing out the open windows, lively dialog about the mission, and even livelier dialog about the upcoming back rubs.

It turns out this type of vehicle is perfect for conditions in and around Clark Air Base. You want something basic, something hearty, something rustic. (Translation: "Rustic" equals "rusty.") You want something that can take a hit, or more accurately, can take a lot of hits. You want a vehicle that features existing scratches and dents. You want something already broken in. Our car fit the bill.

I came to this realization as we drove through the gate and entered the town of Angeles City. The contrast was intense. The simplest way to describe the transition is this: we left the colorful world of Clark Air Base and entered the black and white world of Angeles City. It's as if I was in a Technicolor movie and then—as soon as we drove through the exit gate—the film went to black and white.

The manicured lawns, the carefully trimmed plants and trees, the newly painted buildings, and the well-maintained structures were gone, left back on Clark Air Base. Once the vehicle exited the base, we entered a new world.

Angeles City had the texture of grey. All space was filled with some kind of man-made material, mostly concrete—the sidewalks, the streets, and the buildings. Power lines ran willy-nilly over our heads like they were installed by a seamstress with a serious drug problem. Converted World War II jeeps called "jeepneys" cluttered the streets. The jeepneys were loud. Their engines roared but the loud sound didn't correspond with any burst of power or speed. They didn't go very fast and many of them were not moving at all, waiting for passengers or stuck in traffic.

The next most prominent vehicles on the road were sidecar motorcycles called "trikes." They looked like they were built to hold two extra passengers besides the driver, but I counted five passengers on one of them. Something told me they could probably carry more.

The streets were cluttered with people and vehicles, most not moving.

I would feel extremely nervous driving a brand-new car around Angeles City. The chances of a brand-new car looking brand new after twenty minutes on the streets of Angeles City were near zero. But that's only if I was driving. I must admit, the drivers appeared to be amazingly competent, and I didn't notice any accidents or mishaps during my entire time in the Philippines. So, maybe it all comes down to my perception. Maybe a brand-new car would hold up just fine. Personally, I wouldn't be game to risk it!

I had entered another world—a world of wonder, a world of adventure, a world where the rules are unknown, a world where my previous life experience may not do me much good. I held on. I wanted to find out where this was going to lead.

The car stopped, the doors popped open, and we walked single file into the shop. I stood next to the cash register desk and thought, "Boy, this room is small."

"Hello, sir. Please lie down here, and I'll be with you in a moment." The young girl talked with a very nice sounding foreign accent. I soon discovered she had the standard Filipino English accent, very distinctive and very easy to understand.

Jim explained the procedure: "Sean, undress to your skivvies and lie on the bed." It wasn't really a bed, more like a doctor's exam table with a comfortable cushion. I was soon in my skivvies, lying face down—eyes closed—on the table.

I was completely relaxed as I started taking in my new environment. The sounds and smells were strange, new, and exciting. I listened intently to the "clack-clack" of the ladies' conversations. I wanted to know what they were talking about. But there was no chance. It sounded like a room full of canaries chirping away. They talked with supreme confidence, knowing the "Americanos" had no idea what they were saying. Their conversation was safe. They could say whatever they wanted with no fear of getting caught out. They could have been saying "I love you, GI" or "I'll stab you, GI" and we would never know. But somehow I felt at ease. Jim was a frequent customer, and the girls seemed to know him and like him. I felt like I was in good hands (no pun intended). But you just never know.

The room had a most amazing smell—the smell of relaxation. It was the burning of some exotic incense. But I could detect a mix of far-off cooking smells that complemented it well. It was like the collision of burning incense, rice, fish, pork, beef, chicken, and spices all blended together. I'd never smelled it before, but I liked it immediately. It put me in a good mood, a trusting mood, a worry-free mood. I was enjoying the moment. I became focused on the now.

Her hands started rubbing my neck and shoulders. Prior to her touching me, I don't think I ever had a back rub. I entered new territory—the territory of the pampered. I started feeling guilty. I wasn't used to such luxury. The guilt quickly went away as the lady continued to rub out all my worries and cares. My mind cleared and made room for only one thought—relaxation. All other thoughts were banished. All other thoughts were outlawed. All other thoughts were forgotten.

I continued to enjoy this other-world experience for about thirty minutes. Then I headed back to planet earth.

"How did you like that, Sean?" Jim asked as we stood around the counter waiting to pay. "Not bad for two bucks, eh?"

I just smiled and nodded. I was still on my way back to earth.

"Thank you, Jim. Bring your friend again next time. We like him," said the pretty girl behind the counter taking the money.

"Sorry, Tessie. He's only in town for a couple of weeks. He's just visiting."

We all piled back into the rust bucket and left a big cloud of black smoke in our wake.

As I sat in the back seat looking out at the grey scenery, I thought to myself, "The trip to the Philippines was worth it just for that back rub!"

* * *

The rusty jalopy came to a halt in a parking spot outside a nondescript building on base. The car doors flew open and we headed inside.

"Sean, I got to show you the NCO (noncommissioned officer) club. Best lunch deals and a lot of other bonuses you'll never find anywhere else. Come on, you've got to see this." Jim sold me on lunch at the NCO club.

We entered the main lobby area and got stuck. The place was packed. People going back and forth and others - like us - standing around. I remember my eyes locking onto something that was, shall we say, very interesting. One of Jim's barracks buddies had gone off to reserve a table for our group. In the meantime we would mull around this big lobby or entertainment area. I wasn't in a hurry to leave. I would have been happy to have lunch served to me in the lobby and eat it standing up.

Why?

Because I didn't want to stop staring at the "something" that was very "interesting!"

I couldn't believe what I was seeing. I don't think anyone else in the packed room even noticed. They were unimpressed. It reminded me of when I'd go to a seaside town and stare at the ocean. All the locals think I'm nuts. The locals see the ocean every day; no big deal. But for me, it's a very big deal. I could stare at it for hours on end.

Well, I was getting that seaside feeling inside the NCO club as I stared at the beautiful ladies prancing on a slightly raised stage off to the side. These gorgeous gals were wearing very skimpy bathing suits. I wasn't used to seeing beautiful, nearly naked women walking or dancing to loud music in the afternoon during my lunch break. This was new for me, not an everyday occurrence.

But from the blasé reaction of the others in the room, I got the impression what I was seeing was an everyday occurrence. The show was just a normal part of the operation. No big deal—happens every day. I tried to act cool, but I couldn't do it. My constant glances towards the stage must have given me away. I had to blink to make sure I wasn't seeing things. It seemed so inappropriate, yet I couldn't (wouldn't?) stop looking.

As I continued staring at the beautiful local ladies, I heard someone call out, "Hey, what are you doing here?"

I looked, but only as a curious gesture. And I felt silly responding because I didn't know anybody at Clark Air Base except my tech-school friend Jim, and I'd already bumped into him. So, it was just a knee-jerk reaction.

But when I saw her, my pose changed abruptly. I went from cool, calm, and collected to my best "deer in the headlights" impression.

She looked straight at me and continued talking. "Well I'll be, Lieutenant Mitchell. I've been watching since you came in and wanted to make sure it was you before coming over and harassing you. What brings you to Clark Air Base?"

I collected myself the best I could. I was stunned. I knew her, all right. We were both in the Catholic young-adults group back at Lowry. I liked her. She was a great gal, great personality, fun to be around.

"Chrisa, so good to see you! What am I doing here? What are you doing here?"

"I'm stationed here. I put in for the Philippines and got it. This is my home for the next two years. So, now you tell me, why are you here?"

"I just hitched a ride out from Hawaii and Guam. Plane dropped me off here. Wow, it's great to see you!"

"Great to see you too!" she exclaimed. "It's crazy seeing you in this place; I never expected to see you here. What a total surprise."

It made sense for Chrisa to be stationed in the Philippines. She's Filipino. She looked 100 percent Filipino but acted 100 percent Americano. She spoke perfect LA (Los Angeles) English. And why not, she was born and raised in LA.

She was a very pretty young lady. She had short stylish black hair, beautiful brown complexion, matching brown eyes, long slender legs, and to top it all off—a gorgeous toothpaste commercial quality smile. Did I mention she was full of life? She radiated positive energy, giving off an uplifting force field. She had the power to cheer people up. I'll bet she could crack the toughest cases—the saddest folks. She could probably bring a smile to the second place contestants at the Oscars—she's that good!

She was only nineteen years old.

I couldn't believe my good fortune bumping into Chrisa half way around the world. I really wanted to hang out with her and talk about the "old" days at Lowry. "I'm here with an old friend from tech school. We're having lunch. Want to catch up some other time for a coffee?"

She took out a piece of paper and pen and started writing, "I'm in the barracks. It's the hallway phone. Just call, and someone will come get me. Or you can catch me at work—here's my work number."

We said our good-byes, and I headed for the dining area. As I walked away, my eyes, once again, locked on like a heat-seeking missile to the gorgeous bathing-suit dancing ladies. While talking to Chrisa, I'd forgotten the ladies were there. But now they were back on the radar. I figured I might as well enjoy the scenery. There's no way I was going to see anything this exciting at the chow hall back in Denver.

5. THE BARRACKS

Sorry, Lieutenant Mitchell, but we won't know if we have any rooms available for another hour or so," said the young lady behind the counter. "If you come back in an hour, I may be able to tell you.

I was getting tired of this daily ritual. I would get up in the morning, clean up, and then pack my bags and head to the Chambers Hall lobby. Then I'd have my bags locked up for the day while I explored the area. In the afternoon I'd come back and see if they had a room available for that evening.

This was my third day, and I wanted out of this routine. I wanted a more "permanent" temporary living arrangement.

"I'm wondering—is there another place on base I could stay? Somewhere I don't have to keep checking in everyday to see if I can get a room?"

I hated to leave my elegant accommodation, but I'd swap it gladly for a place I could call my own for the next week or so.

The lady didn't tell me what I wanted to hear. "Sorry, but Chambers Hall is the only officer quarters on base. The only other option is to stay off base."

"I just want to get out of coming in here every day looking for a room. I don't mind something more basic as long as I don't have to keep doing this every day."

A man stepped out from the back area onto the scene. He'd been listening to our conversation. "We have plenty of rooms available over in the visiting airman quarters. If you don't mind staying there, we can get you in for as long as you want."

My eyes got big—huge—as I cheerfully accepted this offer. "Sounds great; let's do it."

"OK, sir; let me get the form." He wandered into the back area and then came out holding a form. The military has a form for everything. "Sign here to say that you have voluntarily accepted a lower room standard. We can't book you in the enlisted quarters unless you sign this form. Otherwise, we get in trouble. Officers are not meant to stay in the enlisted quarters."

I had to smile as I quickly signed the form. How ridiculous. What a waste of a form. What nonsense. By requesting the room and paying for it, haven't I essentially volunteered to stay there? Why is there a separate form to sign? Makes no sense. I came half way across the world thinking I could somehow outrun the bureaucracy. No chance.

I picked up my bag and darted out the front door. I hailed the next taxi and zoomed off to the other side of the base and my new home—the visiting airman's quarters, affectionately known in military circles as the VAQ.

The taxi stopped. I opened the door, paid the driver two US dollars and then walked up to my new living arrangement. "Hey, this is more my style," I thought as I gazed upon a familiar sight—regular old GI barracks. I opened the door to my assigned room and immediately felt at home—a bed, a desk, and a closet. Toilets and showers located down the hallway. I got excited as I now had a permanent home—no more looking for shelter every afternoon.

* * *

"Where you guys coming in from?" I asked the group of four new arrivals to the VAQ. They just moved in, might as well get to know them, welcome them to the neighborhood.

"We're in from Okinawa. Ground crew, we look after the planes. Here on a big exercise for a week," replied one of them.

They looked like a pretty laid-back bunch. Yeah, you could tell they were in the military by their clean-cut appearance, but they had a swagger. They wore their hair at the "outer edge" of the regulation. Long front bangs, hair almost touching the ears and a block cut at the neck line—typical aircrew look, Hollywood-movie-type characters.

I immediately liked these guys. They had a sense of competence about them. They seemed confident in their roles, like they were the best of the best, the A-team, personally selected to be on this special assignment. The JV team and the B-squad were back in Okinawa...at least that's what I envisioned.

I guess that's one of the things I really liked about folks who worked in the "flying" air force. They seemed more concerned about getting the job done than worrying about military tradition. They seemed more focused on getting the mission accomplished—whatever it takes. They're not worried about looking pretty or following stupid mission-killing rules. They're into getting it done...skip the fanfare...do it. I love that attitude. It motivates me. I felt motivated by these guys.

We were all hanging out in the back of the barracks, some leaning up against the handrail and some sitting on the concrete with legs dangling. I continued my line of questioning.

"So, how do you like being in the air force?"

I got smacked with a verbal backhand.

"We ain't in no air force! We're marines!"

I was floored. I'd seen marines. These guys didn't look anything like marines. They looked like typical air-force maintenance troops. OK, not typical. They looked sharp and in great physical condition, but they still had that laid-back air-force look. So, I just figured they were part of some elite air-force maintenance team.

I pressed forward with my line of questioning.

"What's with the long hair?" I asked bravely, half expecting to get invited to my very own GI blanket party.

"Oh yeah, we get that all the time. Well, we're in the flying marine corps. We're different. We're not into all that "hoo-rah" stuff. We just get the job done. And folks leave us alone. We know our stuff so the brass doesn't mess with us. We're hard to replace. We been at this a long time and the pilots trust us; they don't want anyone else, so we get away with a lot. We don't get treated like the average grunt. That's what makes being in the air wing so great. We get to be marines, but we don't have to put up with a lot of the crap."

I knew there was something special about this group. They were marines—long-haired marines—but marines none the less. And I liked them. I respected them. I was proud to be hanging out with them.

What this exchange taught me is aircrew folks are generally the same. Troops who work on aircraft—regardless of service—have a similar attitude. They tend to ignore all the side BS, the red tape—the nonsense. They focus on the work. I respect that.

6. BILLY BONG

G imme peso! Gimme peso!" exclaimed the young boy. He looked about ten years old, hard to tell. Confident, tough, and persistent, he seemed street wise beyond his years. He dressed in normal Angeles City street-kid attire—shorts, T-shirt, flip flops, and a big friendly smile. I liked him. But I didn't like what he was doing. I didn't go for his line of work. I figured an enterprising, energetic, business-minded young lad could do a lot better than running after people begging them for money.

It was just after sunset on the streets of Angeles City. I was out "exploring" with my tech school buddy Jim and a few of his friends from the dorm.

"That's BB. Just give him a peso, and he'll go away," said Jim. I watched as Jim and the other guys started handing over pesos to the young man. Apparently, BB was well-known and popular among the guys from the base.

I thought to myself, "Wow, another crazy Filipino name!" I couldn't resist, so I asked, "Where'd you come up with the name BB?"

This is when I found out I was dealing with a junior lawyer. BB launched into a formal explanation. He talked as if he was really proud of his nickname. He sounded like some American bragging about tracing his heritage back to the Pilgrims. I was stunned by his command of English. His "gimme peso" battle cry threw me off, made me think he didn't know much English, but, when he suddenly turned into a street lawyer, the game was up.

I listened intently as BB explained, "My real name is Billy, which is short for William. But my nickname is Bong. There are so many guys called Bong, it got too confusing so I became Billy Bong, which got shortened to BB. I go by Billy Bong or BB, take your pick."

My follow-up question had nothing to do with his explanation. But curiosity got me again, and I had to ask, "How did you learn to speak English so well?"

"Been hanging out with GIs. I learned from you guys."

"I'm jealous," I said.

"Why?"

"'Cause your English is soooo gooood, and my Tagalog is soooo baaaad!"

BB and I had a good laugh.

Even though BB was winning me over, I wasn't giving him a peso. I wasn't giving him anything. I figured that was a surefire way to ruin the kid. I had to admire his persistence when he wouldn't give up. He kept following me around the streets of Angeles City with his same sales pitch, "Gimme peso!"

"Sean, give the kid a peso, or he'll chase you all over town," Jim exhorted. "It's the only way to get rid of him."

I wanted to get rid of young BB, but I didn't want to contribute to his downfall—I didn't want to be part of the problem. I didn't want to support his "asking for money" business. So I came up with an idea, a plan.

"Gimme peso! Gimme peso!" Billy's voice got louder and more urgent as he struggled to get his message heard over the street noise and our lively group conversation.

"Come on, pal, give him a peso and be done with it—you can't be that cheap?" said one of Jim's buddies from the barracks.

I ignored this useless input and turned to face my little salesman. That's when I put my plan into action. I stooped over slightly, looked BB in the eye, held out my right palm and said, "You give me peso!"

BB froze. He stood as still as a block of ice. His frozen expression is still fresh in my memory. His Filipino eyes became as huge and as round as two large pizzas. His mouth opened wide enough for a dentist to operate. His arms and legs were stretched out to the side as if half way in the middle of a gesture—as if he'd been sprayed by Mr. Freeze.

I repeated my sales pitch slowly, with conviction and with my best attempt at a Filipino accent, "I want you to give me peso!"

I waited for his response. I wondered what he was going to do. I thought he might argue with me. His argument may be simple, as simple as repeating his sales pitch and ignoring my request. Maybe he would launch into a street lawyer argument and embarrass the hell out of me in front of the gathered crowd. Maybe he would kick dirt on my shoes. Maybe he'd call me names. I wasn't sure. But I had executed my plan. My plan was simple—turn the tables. Ask him for a peso and see how he reacts. Might be good for him to hear it coming back the other way—what it sounds like. Let's see what he does.

I got my answer very quickly.

Without saying a word, Billy Bong broke his frozen pose, turned, and rocketed away. He ran at top speed. How fast? Well, I'd say he ran as fast as an Olympic sprinter...no, wait a minute...faster than that—as fast as a high-speed train...no, hold on...even faster— almost as fast as a politician running away from his campaign promises! All that remained of BB was a swirling cloud of street dust.

Jim and the guys were not happy with my approach. "Good job. You chased him away. Bet you feel real good right now, all for a lousy peso. Why didn't you just give the kid a peso—what's wrong with you?"

"That kid's our buddy. We look after him. Now you chased him away. He'll probably never talk to us again. What did you go and do that for?"

I wasn't having any of it. "Look, if you guys want to promote begging, that's your business, but I'm not going to support it. I don't want to ruin the kid. You guys want to ruin him, fine, but don't ask me to do it."

Jim seemed to accept my defense. He seemed to accept my logic. But I don't think I won any points with the other guys.

Later that evening...

The San Miguel beer tasted great. And they were cheap—thirty pesos per bottle. That's less than one US dollar a beer. And the food was superb—delicious and inexpensive.

We left the restaurant and stood in the dirt backstreet planning our next move. Some guys wanted to go to one place; others wanted somewhere else. I wasn't so fussed. I just wanted to explore. Get to know the heartbeat of this exotic locale—this new world. I felt so alive. It seemed like adventure lurked around every corner. Every few steps, I'd see something I'd never seen before.

As the discussion raged about our next destination, I felt a tug on the back left side of my shorts. I quickly turned to look, and there stood young Billy Bong. He held out his open palm showcasing a shiny peso.

"I got your peso!"

Now it was my turn to get sprayed by Mr. Freeze. I was stunned. My plan caused a reaction I never anticipated. I never expected to see Billy Bong again. I thought the little guy hated me for what I'd done. But now it was my turn to be shocked. I snapped out of it and replied, "You keep it."

BB's smile went from large to extra-large as he said, "Thanks!" He clamped his hand tightly around the peso and ran off into the crowded Angeles City streets.

BB won me over. I liked this enterprising young lad. I wondered if I'd ever see him again.

7. THE GYM

I never go off base," said my new acquaintance. "Been stationed here for over a year and haven't left the base. Not going to. Good way to get killed."

I was hanging out in a place I felt comfortable, the gym—specifically the weight-lifting area. I would always seek out the gym at a new place as a way to get acclimated. I felt at ease in the gym. It gave me a sense of familiarity—a sense of belonging and a sense of kinship. My usual workout included bench presses, push-ups, pull-ups, and sit ups. I'd do three sets—ten reps each—and then head outside for a twenty to thirty minute run.

My new acquaintance was a solid built young man stationed at Clark and living in one of the enlisted dormitories. We got talking. At first about weightlifting, and then it turned off topic as I wanted to find out more about the base and the local area. I figured he'd be a good source of local information. I was right, but I didn't like what I was hearing.

"A good way to get killed? How do you figure?" I asked like a green recruit going off into battle and not wanting to believe what the veterans were telling me—"War ain't nothing like what you see in the movies. All this hero stuff is just Hollywood crap!"

I listened closely as my workout pal filled me in on the details.

"Couple guys got killed just last month. Shot point blank in the head for no reason. They just wanted to get a couple of GIs. These guys happened to be there so they got it. I ain't going out there. I'm staying right here until my two years are up. Then it's back to the States."

"So, these guys weren't doing anything? Just minding their own business?" I asked in an unbelieving tone.

"Well, there's probably more to it than that. You can't always believe what you read in the base paper. Maybe they were involved in a card game gone bad or even a drug deal that fell through. We got guys on base doing stuff like that. They're crazy. That's insane. But the bottom line is these two guys are dead, shot dead. And they'll never catch the killers, won't happen. We've seen it before; they never catch the killers."

After my new gym buddy finished his "pep talk," I went outside for a jog and to process this new information.

I took in the beautiful scenery. I jogged around the parade grounds. I stopped to read the plaque marking the site of the old army post— Fort Stotsenburg. The plaque and the beautiful parade ground brought to mind a book I read, *General Wainwright's Story*. I picked it up at the Lowry Base Library. They were getting rid of old books. I think they just gave it to me—no charge. The book is a World War II story about the fall of the Philippines in early 1942. Wainwright was the commanding officer who surrendered the islands to the Japanese.

As I looked over the parade grounds, I imagined cavalry horses galloping about with fancy-dressed soldiers riding smartly in precision formation. In his book, Wainwright talks about the fondness he feels for his horse and how it broke his heart to kill it. The troops were starving. He gave the order, "Kill the horses." His beloved horse would be first. For some reason that part of his story hit me the hardest. I'm not really a horse lover or have ever had much to do with horses, but I felt his pain. I wondered how he could do it. But I guess that's war. If the troops are starving, you find a way to feed them. If it means killing the horses, then do it. For some reason, this is what I thought about as I gazed upon the beautiful Fort Stotsenburg parade ground.

I admired the manicured grass, the beautiful flowers, the majestic trees, and the serenity. I remember the quiet. I felt like I was the only person on base. It seemed strange because the base was in full tempo with lots of people. But I suppose I was the only person willing to go for a jog at midafternoon during probably the hottest time of day. As such, I got the parade grounds to myself.

My jogging session calmed me down and gave me new confidence. I discounted the terror-filled input I received from my new gym pal. I decided—unlike him—I would be going off base, I would be exploring, and I would be venturing out into the Philippine unknown.

8. GATE GUARDS

How do you like your job?" I asked the gate guards. There were two of them, both Filipino. I was standing on the left side of the gate as you look out from the base. I was waiting for a cab. I figured I'd start up a conversation.

"It's OK, sir," replied one of them. I could tell they were a bit hesitant about talking to me. I was in civilian clothes so they weren't sure what sort of courtesy to extend me. I knew the feeling well. A military-looking guy in civilian clothes could be just about any rank, so best to err on the side of caution. The guard used caution when he called me *sir*. But he didn't have to. I'm standing there in baggie white shorts, a loose collared shirt, and a camera strap over my shoulder. I looked like a tourist. I'm OK if he treats me like one.

I wanted to talk to these troops. They looked sharp. Their weapons slung over their shoulders as they held on with one hand to the strap in front. They were clean cut and, as I would find out, very well spoken.

"What do you like most about it?" I continued probing.

The guards looked at each other as if a married couple deciding who's going to answer the embarrassing game show question.

Finally, one of them spoke up, "I like the pay." Then he quickly added, "But we don't make much compared to the Americans. We do the same job but get paid much less. It creates problems."

"What kind of problems?" I inquired.

"Big problems; there's lots of fights. We get sick of seeing the Americans acting like they're better than we are; acting like they're our boss—we hate it."

"Fights? Really? Where? Between who?" I stammered.

"Everywhere, guys fighting all the time, in the chow hall, back at the dorms; heck, yesterday we even had a fight right here at the gate. An American guard started yelling at a Filipino guard. The Filipino got angry and belted the American. The American was much bigger, but after getting hit in the face, he just backed off. Both guys were held back anyway, but the American didn't want any part of a fight. Both guys got suspended, but it left us all very tense. Now, it's like an us- versus-them situation. We stick to our side, they stick to theirs.

"There's bad blood between us. It's too bad 'cause some of the American guards are nice guys, but they're not allowed to fraternize with us anymore. But there's a few of them who are really bad troublemakers. They treat us like dirt. The look down on us; they think they're better than us. Right here in our own country. This is the Philippines, not the United States, yet these guys think they own us. I'm sick of it; we're all sick of it."

I was floored by this revelation. I quickly looked across the way at the two American guards. They carried presidential poses like stage actors trying to not look our way, as if our side of the street was a "no-look" zone. I was amazed at how they wouldn't acknowledge my gaze. I had a strange feeling they viewed me as the bad guy for hanging out on the Filipino side—aiding and abetting the enemy.

I started feeling awkward, like I was standing in no-man's-land between the Hatfield's and McCoy's.

The taxi pulled up; I hopped in and waved good-bye to the Filipino gate guards. I looked over to the American guards in order to wave, but they were busy dealing with some people leaving the base.

9. DINA

Hello, I'm Sean," I said to the lady sitting to my right. I sat in the last stool before the counter took a hard ninety-degree turn away from me and in front of her. We were more or less the only people at the bar. Most everyone else was sitting or standing at the nearby tables.

She smiled and replied, "Hi, Sean. I'm Dina (pronounced Dee-nah), nice to meet you." Even if she didn't tell me her name, I could have figured it out by leaning forward a bit to read the ID card hanging from a lanyard around her neck. I found the card a distraction. I felt a little uncomfortable talking to a lady with an ID card on display. I tried to ignore it. Jim filled me in on the card thing. All the bar-girls wore them to show they were "clean"—no venereal disease.

I liked her. She seemed very nice and personable. I listened to her conversation with my tech school buddy Jim for the last few minutes, and she impressed me. She knew Jim; they were friends. I can't remember if she was beautiful or not. I just remember her friendliness, her openness, her sincerity.

"So, how do you know Jim?" I asked.

"He's been coming here for a long time. He's a good guy. Not all the guys are nice like Jim."

"Some of the guys are not so nice, huh?" I wanted her to tell me more. Her assertion made me curious.

"Yeah, some of the guys can be mean. They take advantage of us. They think 'cause they have money, they can boss us around. They can do whatever they want. But Jim's not like that. He's nice. He treats me and the other girls really well. He's a friend."

"Are you from Angeles City?" I got off the topic. I wasn't ready to hear any specifics of just how mean the GIs could be.

"No, I'm from Cebu, a long way from here, in the central Philippines. Have you been to Cebu?"

"No. But I'd like to go someday and explore some of the other islands too."

"It's beautiful there. I miss it. I miss my family, my mom, dad, and brothers and sisters—all my relatives and friends. I send money home every month. I'm looking forward to going home for good after I make enough money. I've been here for two years now; I figure another two years and I'll have enough to quit. That's when I'll go home for good."

Just then we were interrupted by a guy who looked like a typical GI from the base. And something told me he was acting like a typical one too as he snapped at Dina, "You bitch. You think you can just brush me off. Forget it. I'm gonna get you fired. I bought you two drinks, and now you gonna ignore me? Not happening!"

I quickly perched up in my bar stool, ready to take action if it got any crazier. And it did get crazier, but Dina didn't need any help from me. She demonstrated her prowess. She let him have it.

"Shut up! Get away from me—Now! Beat it!"

Then she added a powerful word that settled it for good, a word that sent the bullying GI packing with his tail between his legs, a word that wounded him worse than a bullet to the chest, a word that put him in his place—a word that summed up his behavior.

She looked up at him with a steely eyed stare and finished him off with her one word death shot.

"Loser!"

I was astonished as the "loser" turned and drifted away like a wobbly legged boxer walking to his corner after fifteen rounds of head shots.

Then Dina calmly turned back to me and asked, "So, what brings you to the Philippines, Sean? Are you stationed here at Clark?"

I liked this gal. I liked her attitude. I liked her boldness, her bravery, her strength.

We talked for about thirty minutes. I felt like I got some insights into the "bar girl" situation as I probed for answers to understand why it is ... the way it is.

I'll relay what Dina told me.

"I want to meet a nice American and get married, although it's not easy to find a nice man here. It seems like most of the GIs want one thing and one thing only. And many of them are very rude and mean. I hate that. I would like to find a man, fall in love, and then get married. That's what I want, and that's what most of the girls here want. That's the dream. But unfortunately, very few girls get married. And even when they do, it can be even worse. Some of the guys may seem nice at first, but then they turn into monsters. I'd like to find a really nice guy, a guy who's sincere. Not one of these monsters."

I listened. I observed. She spoke with conviction. I believed her.

I continued. "Why an American? Why not a Filipino?"

She was prepared for that question.

"Americans have money. Even the lowest ranking GI is rich by Filipino standards. The salary of the lowest ranking GI can support several families here in the Philippines. Filipinos make hardly any money, even doctors and nurses. College graduates make less than a two-striper GI."

I got the truth. Now I knew she wasn't feeding me a line. It comes down to economics. And the universal rule of economics—No money; no honey!

Jim had stepped away from the bar to socialize but came back to let me know it was time to move on. I said good-bye to Dina. The interview was over.

10. ANTONIO

I discovered my new home at the enlisted visitors' barracks was a local hangout. Some of the base workers would gather around the back area for smoking and socializing, catching up on the latest. I joined them one late afternoon.

"So, what language are you speaking?" I asked trying to work my way into the conversation. There were about ten of us gathered along the concrete exit ramp.

I directed my question to Antonio because we had been talking earlier, and I felt most comfortable with him.

"Pampanga," answered Antonio, "but most of the time it's Tagalog." He spoke with a friendly authoritative tone, if there is such a combination. His deep commanding voice gave him instant credibility. He told me he was forty years old but he could have passed for much younger. He was a little shorter than my six-foot frame but towered over the other Filipino workers.

Antonio came across as a natural leader. He had a dominating presence. I felt like I was talking to someone who knew the game and knew what was going on—someone in control.

Communicating with Antonio—and the other Filipino workers—was easy. Their English was superb. I made no attempt to slow down or change my delivery. I understood them; they understood me.

"Why Pampanga?"

"It's the local dialect. But it's better if we speak Tagalog, the national language. All Filipinos speak Tagalog.

Someone jumped into the conversation. "Except Ilocanos; can't understand a word they say."

Antonio agreed. "Yeah, true. Ilocanos try to speak to us in Tagalog, but it's no use. You know what we tell them?"

I stood there with a puzzled look as I pondered this rhetorical question.

Antonio delivered the punch line.

"Speak English!"

Everyone except me started laughing. I didn't catch the humor. They found it hysterical. I think it went over my head because I'm just a one-language person. Most everyone else at the gathering spoke at least three languages. First would be their local language, then the national language, Tagalog, and finally English. I was the only "one talk" person.

Antonio continued with his explanation. "The Ilocanos speak crooked Tagalog. It's so difficult to understand them. If they start speaking Tagalog, we just tell them to speak English."

I changed the subject. I figured this was a great opportunity to learn even more about the Philippines. "I've got a group of locals right here, right now. What can I find out?" I felt brave. I dove into the forbidden topic—politics.

"Hey, now that Cory is your new president, how's everything going? Is it better under Cory than it was under Marcos?"

Cory Aquino had been in office a few years. I heard great things in the news about her administration. I wanted to hear it from the folks on the ground.

They told me. But it wasn't what I expected.

"It's worse!" Someone bellowed from across the concrete ramp.

"Yeah, it's worse. Bring Marcos back," chimed in another.

I was surprised. I thought everything in the Philippines was going great. People Power was the rage, rise of the common person, land reforms, and all the other good news stories. Of course, my only source of information was the mainstream newspapers and television, so I should have known better. But still I wondered how my impression could be so far off. The response was 180 degrees opposite from what I'd heard in the so-called news.

I had to fire off some follow-on questions.

"I thought Cory was bringing in People Power? I thought she was going to get rid of corruption? I thought she was going to bring about land reforms and end bribery?"

"Are you kidding? Corruption is worse now. Bribery is worse. And land reforms? Cory's idea of land reform is to take it from you and give it to her cronies. It's worse now than it ever was under Marcos."

I'm glad I asked because I was getting insights I'd never get from reading the newspaper or watching the television news. I've always found it better to talk to the people. The people know. They know what's going on. These guys were giving me the straight skinny. They weren't pulling any punches. I appreciated it.

I wondered if the main stream media is this far off about Filipino politics, then are they reporting anything accurately? Are they just simply getting it wrong or—could it be something much more sinister—like they're lying?

Either way, this was a point in my life where I started to question what I see, hear, and read from the mainstream media.

Now it was Antonio's turn to change the subject when he asked me, "Are you going to be doing any sightseeing while you're here in the Philippines?"

"Oh yeah, I'm off to Baguio tomorrow, taking the bus. It leaves from Kelly Cafeteria at eight a.m., looking forward to it."

"Going to Camp John Hay?" Antonio asked.

"That's right. Have you been there? Is it nice?"

"Been there lots of times. We go up there every couple of months to carry out some maintenance. We make extra money on those trips. Everyone volunteers for that duty. And the place is gorgeous. Not a blade of grass out of place. Baguio is the summer capital of the Philippines. People flock there to escape the lowland heat, so you better bring a jacket."

I silently questioned Antonio's judgment. "Bring a jacket to Baguio? Why? Even if it's twenty degrees cooler than Angeles City, it would still be too hot for a jacket. A twenty-degree drop would put the temperature around sixty-eight degrees Fahrenheit—room temperature. Nah, I don't need a jacket." I discounted his advice. And I would later pay the price.

11. BAGUIO

I grabbed a seat and a cup of coffee at Kelly Cafeteria. Then I waited for the bus. I looked down at my ticket—Clark Air Base to Camp John Hay in Baguio City. I was excited and ready to go.

Baguio, the summer capital of the Philippines. It's where you go to get relief from the heat. It's up in the highlands of Benguet Province.

It sure was hot down in the lowlands of Angeles City and Clark Air Base. And the locals were pretty creative when it came to beating the heat. I visited the Base Exchange—affectionately and commonly known as the BX—and saw something for the first time; local ladies walking around with umbrellas in full bloom up over their heads as if anticipating a rainstorm. This looked so odd to me because there wasn't a cloud in the sky, just the baking sun. Then it dawned on me, "Them umbrellas are perfect sun blockers!" I watched as these clever ladies walked about in a leisurely and carefree manner, not at all bothered by the scorching sun. On the other hand, I would scurry from shady spot to shady spot to escape the penetrating sun beams.

The umbrellas were great for blocking out the sun, but they did nothing for blocking out the humidity. You couldn't hide from the humidity. Shade would stop me from getting sunburned but it did nothing to stop me from sweating. Sweat dripped off my body like water spilling over Niagara Falls. The only relief from the heat was to duck inside the nearest air-conditioned building.

But my attitude about the heat was—so what? Wear shorts, a loose shirt, comfortable deck shoes and continue exploring. A body soaked with sweat is no reason to complain or stop the adventure.

All was fine for now. I was in the nice air-conditioned confines of Kelly Cafeteria waiting for the bus that would take me to Baguio, sipping on my coffee and staring at my ticket.

I noticed a base paper sitting at the empty table next to mine. The headline caught my eye, "CIGARETTES DISAPPEAR! 820 CASES! BASE COMMANDER OFFERS REWARD FOR INFORMATION!" I grabbed the paper and started reading.

According to the story, the container was shipped overland from Subic Bay Naval Base. The tamper-proof seal was intact but when they opened the container it was empty. Someone walked off with 820 cases of cigarettes. The street value was through the roof. Someone was out there making a fortune selling black market cigarettes. The base commander was offering a reward for information about who did it.

As I read the story, I could feel the commander's pain. The heist made him look foolish. I can see someone making off with the whole container, but how did they get into the sealed container, walk off with all the contents, and then reseal it as if never opened? It had all the markings of an inside job.

I flipped further through the newspaper pages and another story jumped out at me, "RETIRED AIR FORCE MASTER SERGEANT SHOT DEAD!" He was waiting in the congested Angeles City traffic and a couple of masked gunmen emptied their magazines into the driver-side tinted window. They couldn't even see who they were shooting. According to the story, the killers identified the car as belonging to an American because it was brand new and had that "I'm rich" look. So, they figured it must belong to an American. They were right—sort of. The man they killed was an American, but he was born in the Philippines; his home town—Angeles City. So, they probably would have preferred to kill someone a little *more* American than the person they got.

After reading the article, I looked up and thought, "I need to stop reading the base paper—too scary."

I left the air-conditioned confines of Kelly Cafeteria and entered the air-conditioned bus. I grabbed a seat on the left-hand side near the back. Passengers kept loading until most of the seats were filled. I was lucky. When the driver closed the door and pulled away, I still had a seat all to myself. I scooched over to the window, pressed my face against the glass, and focused my eyes outward as I was determined to take in all the sights along the way.

The bus slowed down as we exited through a side gate on the base. A troupe of Filipino soldiers stood lined up as we drove past. I turned my head backward and watched the soldiers swing the gate closed behind us.

As soon as we passed the base boundary wall, my eyes were feasted to a stark contrasting scene. The green grass and manicured gardens were gone. The tidy, well built, good looking buildings were gone. The fancy-dressed umbrella-toting ladies were gone. Instead I was treated to a much more adventurous setting.

I saw houses lined up on both sides of the street. I use the word houses loosely. All were in a state of disrepair, as if construction was halted for some reason or another. The houses were small, with only two or three rooms. Some had rooms added on, and some had second stories, but I remember thinking they looked small.

People were lined up on both sides of the street. I felt like I was in a hometown ticker-tape parade for returning war heroes. I saw what looked like moms and grandmothers and even a few grandfathers in the mix. But mostly the crowd consisted of young kids whooping and carrying on like they were watching a Disneyland parade.

The common denominator among these adoring fans is this—they looked happy. They looked genuinely happy to see us. Or they were just happy period. I don't know. I just remember the happy faces.

As I stared at the jumping happy children through the bus window, my focus was interrupted by a lady's voice. "Do you know what today is?" It was the lady sitting in the seat ahead of me. When I first got on the bus, we had a nice easygoing chat. From our conversation I found out she lived in Sacramento, California, and was out visiting her family in Angeles City. She was taking her niece to Camp John Hay for a visit. The lady looked about forty years old, wore black glasses and—as I would soon find out—was concerned about her and her niece's safety.

I answered her strange question. "No. No idea what today is..."

She shot back in an excited tone, "It's the NPA's birthday."

That meant nothing to me. But she didn't wait for me to respond. Instead she just continued, "And you know what the NPA likes to do on their birthday?"

Again, I was stumped. Again, she continued. "They like to kill people."

The conversation suddenly changed from a light hearted "first time you meet someone" dialog into a serious "we're friends" plea for assistance as she asked, "Will you protect us? Will you look after us in case the bus gets attacked by NPA? I would really appreciate it?"

My attitude took a dive. Here I am, sitting comfortably on a bus headed for Camp John Hay, relaxing, taking it easy, making new friends, and *pow*! I get asked to provide security services. I thought, "This is ridiculous. What am I going to do if the NPA attacks the bus? And who is this NPA anyway? What am I going to do if anybody attacks the bus—especially someone who's armed?"

But I wasn't going to let the lady down. I figured I'd humor her, so I replied, "Sure."

"Thanks so much. We're on our own, and I'm scared about traveling on the NPA's birthday. I'd rather not but this was the only day we had to travel, and I wanted to get to Baguio; I wanted to take my niece. Thanks so much for looking after us."

I had all I could do to keep from laughing. Not at the NPA threat but at the thought of me being a protector of some sort. I felt like changing into a medieval knight's outfit and hiring a white horse for the day.

"So, tell me about these NPA. Who are they?" I asked. After all, the first tenant of the military is—know thy enemy.

She gave me the lowdown. "Stands for New People's Army. They go around attacking people. And they always attack on their birthday which is today. And they like to target buses—especially buses from the base."

This is the first I'd heard of the NPA. I was starting to get over my initial fear as I rationalized to myself, "Come on, I never heard of them; I didn't hear anything on base about it. If the threat was real, they'd never let this bus off the base. I think this lady from California has been watching too much TV and reading too many newspapers. I think she's overreacting. I think she's been away from the Philippines too long and is getting scared by the boogeyman."

I made a decision to discount her scare mongering. I made a decision to enjoy the trip, and if trouble turns up—deal with it then. Besides, what's worrying about it going to do?

I changed the subject: "Oh, by the way, I'm Sean." I then raised my hand with open palm and gave a little wave.

"Hi Sean, my name is Rosita, and this is my niece Tin-Tin. Do you work at the base?"

"No, I'm stationed in Colorado. I'm just here visiting, getting a look at the Philippines. It's my first time here."

We continued talking and I noticed Rosita became more relaxed, more at ease. I guess she figured there's nothing to fear with her new found bodyguard—me—close by.

* * *

I observed a young girl eating an egg. It was very strange to behold. She held the egg shell with both hands and then she went about sucking the juice from the cracked open top end. I watched with the curiosity of a second grader at a puppet show as she slurped the egg juice. She seemed to really enjoy the taste. I'd never seen an egg eaten like that before.

The bus had pulled over for a rest stop, and I just came out of the store. Prior to buying a diet coke and a candy bar, I used the men's room. The men's room was a new experience. First, it wasn't clean. It was smelly. It looked like it had never been cleaned. Nobody seemed to mind. Next, there was no toilet paper. If you want toilet paper, you bring your own.

Now to explain the diet coke and the candy bar. It's my twisted thinking at that time in my life. I'll try to explain the logic—here goes nothing. Well, regular coke has too much sugar in it, so I drank diet coke. But I'd get a candy bar because—well, that's what I wanted, and besides, the lack of sugar in the diet coke allowed for the sugar in the candy bar. Get it? All makes sense now, right? Didn't think so...

The young girl eating the egg interrupted my confused gaze, "Want some?" as she held up the egg and invited me to suck some of the juice.

I felt off-guard by her question, as if I got caught red-handed staring at her for too long. But I was just drawn to this scene. It was strange. I wanted to know more; I figured here's my chance.

"Ah, no thank you. But what is it?"

"It's a local delicacy called balut. It's a duck egg, delicious. You sure you don't want to try it?"

"That's OK. I'm fine."

I would find out later that balut—pronounced bah-loot—is a Filipino favorite. The duck egg has to be cooked just right, for the right length of time, and at the right incubation period to get that perfect balut. This perfect timing means the little duckling is formed—beak, feathers, legs—and they tell me it's delicious. I wasn't game to try.

* * *

As we traveled closer and closer to our destination—Baguio City— the road became narrower and steeper. We were in mountain country. I was sure the roads were steeper, but I could be wrong about narrower. Maybe they just seemed narrower because the mountain cliffs were so high and so steep. The contrast of the tiny road next to the massive mountains was stark—as if the road was just a thin line on the side of the mountain. I would have felt a lot better if the road was, say, ten times wider! But it wasn't.

And this created a dilemma for me—I was scared to death! The view out my window was spectacular—breathtaking mountain scenery. I took it all in with enjoyment until I looked down and saw the bottomless drop into the valley of trees below. I went from being awestruck at the beautiful mountain scenery to being petrified as I looked down the steep deadly cliffs.

I watched the bus driver closely. I wanted to reassure myself he didn't have a death wish. I wasn't having any luck. He had several driving habits that would have gotten him a failing mark if I was his driving instructor. First, he drove way too fast. He drove the curvy mountain roads like an ambulance driver in a rush to get a dying patient to the emergency room. Next, he drove with abandon. As I looked through the windscreen, I would see the road disappear to the right behind the mountain. Straight ahead was nothing but open air and the valley below. I was praying for him to slow down as we approached the right-hand curve in the road. He didn't. Instead he accelerated around the corner. My heart dropped out of my chest as I braced for liftoff—right off the cliff. But to my eternal surprise, the driver simply made the turn gracefully without incident.

I was now thanking God for keeping me alive. I mentally jumped for joy that we'd survived. It was a miracle. Yes, I felt like I just witnessed a miracle, and by the grace of God, we were all saved from imminent death.

Apparently, I was the only one who felt this way. I looked around, expecting to find other passengers ready to celebrate—share the joy of skirting death. But I had no takers. As I searched the bus, I saw generally two behaviors. First, almost everyone was sleeping. Second, those not sleeping were looking out the windows—

expressionless—as if thinking about paying the light bill back home. They were unfazed, uncaring, and unaware that we'd all just escaped certain death.

One couple in particular stood out. In the front seat, right behind the bus driver, sat an older man and woman. If I had to guess, I'd say they were retired farmers from "upstate somewhere USA." I watched them as the bus driver took blind turns at high speed. I watched them as the bus driver seemed to drive off the cliff and then miraculously land safely back on the road again. I watched them as the bus driver would play "chicken" with the jeepneys—he would simply blow his horn continuously until the offending jeepney driver gave way. He never slowed down. He just kept beeping, as if the horn were an invisible snow plow knocking obstacles out of the way with impunity.

It would have been great entertainment if I wasn't so scared.

But the older couple in the front seat gave me courage. They seemed oblivious—like everyone else—to the danger. They seemed oblivious to how we were skirting death at every dangerous turn. They seemed oblivious to what I knew (yes, I was the only one on the bus who realized): we were all lucky to be alive.

I decided to take a hint from this older couple. "Hey, if they're not scared, then why should I be scared? How can I get so worked up when they're so calm? How can I be so worried when they're so relaxed?"

Besides, everyone else on the bus was "A-OK" with the driver's performance. And I have to admit, he was an exceptionally skillful driver. Only an exceptionally skillful driver could manage the high degree of difficulty—death-defying—stunts he pulled off. If "cliff driving" was an Olympic sport, he would have won the gold medal.

I convinced myself our driver was an Olympic gold-medal cliff-driving champion and decided to relax. I also decided it's probably best if I stopped looking. I closed my eyes and went to sleep. The drive became much more pleasant after I fell asleep.

We stopped for another roadside break to use the restrooms and get a bite to eat. I saw my upstate USA farmer couple and approached them. I had to ask, "How are you enjoying the bus ride?"

The old man gave me a big smile and then launched into a story: "We're loving it. This is a dream trip for us. I've been planning this trip for years. I was here last in 1944, during the war. I've been telling my wife about it ever since—how nice the people were to us. How generous they were. I loved my time in the Philippines, and I'll always be grateful for how the people treated us soldiers. I've been meaning to come back but never seemed to get the time to do it. Now that I'm retired, I've got the time. We wouldn't miss this for anything."

I was fascinated by his response. But I still wanted to find out more. I was deeply curious. Not so much about his war experience—but if they were scared sitting up front! Apparently they weren't, but I had to ask, "Are you OK sitting up front? You're not frightened by how fast we're going over these mountain roads?"

The old man schooled me. "C'mon, this is nothing. I remember driving these roads when the Japs were shooting at us. Has anybody been shooting at the bus today?"

I responded to his rhetorical question with a smile.

He continued, "OK then. You should just enjoy the ride. This driver is an expert. Most Filipino drivers are. You never see any accidents. This mountain country is some of the most beautiful in the world. I've been dreaming about coming back and seeing it again—this is the trip of a lifetime."

I quickly agreed, "Yes, it is beautiful."

We got back on the bus, and I watched the old couple as they sat behind the driver, laughing and carrying on like fourth graders on a school field trip. As I watched them confidently enjoying life and not at all worried about the dangerous road, I took heart. Whenever I saw a life-threatening road situation, I just looked at them and told myself, "Hey, if they're not worried, why should I be worried?"

Note: Several years later, I read an article in the *Stars and Stripes* military newspaper titled "BUS GOES OVER CLIFF ON ROAD TO BAGUIO! ALL DEAD!" I looked up and started talking to everyone and anyone around me. "See! I told you! It happens! They lose busses on that road. That could have been me!" My audience thought I was nuts. I didn't care. I felt like I'd cheated death—I survived my bus ride to Baguio.

By the time we reached Camp John Hay the sun had set. I got my room key, threw my gear on the bed and headed out in search of food.

* * *

It was dark. I found myself standing in a long line outside the restaurant. It was Wednesday—Mongolian Barbeque night, apparently a very popular event. The exotic smells crashed into me from all directions. I was already hungry but the delicious aroma of cooking beef, stir fry vegetables, steamed rice, and oriental spices made me all the more ravenous. This was not your typical air-force chow-hall cooking.

The sounds of beef and vegetables hitting the hot frying pan along with the beautiful food fragrance filling the air helped a lot to minimize my discomfort. After a few minutes of standing in line on the road outside the restaurant, I realized I had miscalculated. I was unprepared for my trip. I was a typical tourist making typical assumptions. My big discomfort causing assumption was this—it's boiling hot in Angeles City, therefore it must be boiling hot in Baguio and all over the Philippines for that matter.

Wrong!

I was standing outside at about 7:00 p.m. in Baguio—Camp John Hay to be exact—wearing shorts and a short sleeve shirt. I was cold.

I looked around at my fellow "in-line standers," and they were all wearing warm jackets and sweaters. I was jealous.

I acted tough as I struggled to keep my teeth from clanging together as a normal reaction to uncomfortably cold weather.

Baguio City is in the mountain province of Benquet. It's up high. It's cold, especially when the sun goes down. I learned that lesson the hard way.

My cold Baguio experience reminded me of the time I went to watch the Giants play the Dodgers at Candlestick Park. I was stationed at "Hot as Hell" Sacramento, and we took off for San Francisco. My friends from the base dormitory told me to take a warm jacket, but I refused saying something like, "C'mon, it can't be that cold. It's a hundred and four here in Sacramento—what's the coldest it could be in San Fran? Seventy or even sixty—that's not cold." My New England mentality got me in trouble. I figured it's not cold until the river ices over.

All I remember about the baseball game is this—*I froze!* I felt like an idiot sitting there, teeth chattering, rubbing myself all over trying to get warm. My friends from the barracks had a good laugh.

Standing in line outside the restaurant at Camp John Hay that Wednesday evening brought back cold memories of the baseball game at Candlestick. Although this time I didn't have any barracks buddies laughing at me. Instead, I had a bunch of strangers trying politely to keep from laughing as they looked at the dummy—me—wearing only shorts and a tee shirt.

I finally sat down at my table and started looking at the menu. It gave me something to do. I already knew what I was getting—the Wednesday special, Mongolian Barbeque. As I looked up from my menu that I wasn't really reading, I saw a couple pair of hands waiving at me. It was the lady from the bus, Rosita and her niece Tin-Tin. They were all smiles and calling me over. I went to see what all the excitement was about.

"Are you eating by yourself?" Rosita asked as if there was some kind of law against it.

"Yes." I replied as if talking to the judge and wondering what my sentence was going to be.

"Well, come over here, and sit with us. Join us for dinner."

So, I sat down at their table. I was happy to join them. I was happy she asked me; beats the heck out of eating alone.

"So, Sean, why did you come to the Philippines? If you're not stationed here and you have no relatives, why come here?"

I thought that was a good question. I'm not sure I could answer it, at least not convincingly. I started to ponder some possible responses—

- *"Oh, I got on the wrong plane and came here by accident."*
- *"Well, you see, I'm doing a research paper on the Philippines..."*
- *"I thought this was Canada. You mean to tell me we're not in Canada?"*

But my response was just the truth—goofy, but the truth.

"I had some leave from work and decided to take advantage of the free military flights. I was in Hawaii and saw all the flights going to the Philippines and decided to go. Why not? Never been there before, a bit of adventure, a bit of spice, something different, something out of the ordinary."

She replied, "Well, you're a brave man. I wouldn't recommend coming here unless you know your way around, unless you know the language. It's dangerous. Be careful, OK?"

I mentally gulped at another dangerous, negative input. Of course, this was the same lady who recruited me as her bodyguard for protection against the NPA. I didn't take her warning too seriously.

The meal was delicious. I enjoyed eating with Rosita and Tin-Tin. When it was time to go, Rosita extended another kind gesture. "Sean, here's my number in Angeles City. Call me when you get back to Clark, and I'll have my nephew pick you up and bring you over the house for a nice Filipino style meal, OK?"

I was very OK. I took the ripped piece of paper and stashed it carefully in my wallet.

* * *

I was awoken by the sunbeam coming through the window. I opened my eyes and stared at the window. I remember lying in bed admiring the scene. The large window frame was white with white wooden separators holding the six or so crystal clear panes of glass. The white sheer curtains looked elegant as they welcomed the warm sunshine into the room. I admired this scene for what seemed like a long time. I didn't want it to end. It was so peaceful. I felt out of place in such an elegant setting. I imagined myself dying and going to heaven and this is what God's waiting room looks likes. "Hey, maybe I died last night?"

As I became more awake, I realized I was very much alive and somehow landed this awesome hotel room. I knew it was nice—I saw it the night before when I checked in, but it looked so much nicer now in the morning sunlight. The aspect that separated this room from all the other hotel rooms I stayed in is this—it was elegant. It had the look of royalty, like someone put care and love into the interior decorating. I'm not much for noticing such things, but this room had such a feeling of elegance that even I sensed it. I wasn't used to it. I was used to an interior decoration style known as "early army barracks." This was an unexpected change. And I appreciated it.

The room at Chambers Hall back at Clark Air Base was very nice, but not this nice. This room took style to a new level.

I walked past the brand-new looking wicker chair and fancy oriental chair into the plush bathroom to relieve myself and brush my teeth. I almost felt guilty messing up this General MacArthur grade accommodation. I wondered if they made a mistake at check-in—I told them I was only a lieutenant!

I got suited up for a jog—shorts, tee shirt, and running shoes. I tucked the room key into my shoe and then opened the elegant white door to enter the outside world.

Once I stepped outside, I was overcome again. I was just beginning to accept the elegance of my hotel room, and now I was faced with another moment of astonishment. As I scanned my setting, I began to have second thoughts—"Maybe I did die last night, and this is heaven!"

The scene was breathtaking.

I saw a wall of exotic trees. Some looked familiar—green bushy tops—most looked foreign, like I was on some other life-supporting planet in another galaxy. I looked with a confused expression at big leafy trees—trees with large and small fruits hanging off. There appeared to be a barely visible forest net of some unknown material connecting all the vegetation. The forest seemed alive. Not alive in a vegetation sense, but alive in an animal sense, almost like it was watching me. There was some kind of a life force reaching out to me. I could feel its presence. I liked it.

I noticed a curving stone wall marking the border of the hotel roundabout drop-off and parking area. I was drawn to a part of the wall where the forest line disappeared. Instead of a mass of forest, there was a gentle blanket of fog. I wondered if there was an open field behind the wall. I wanted to know why there were no tall trees behind that section of the wall.

As I looked out over the wall through the fog, I could see mountains off in the distance. It was a view for the ages. I shook my head wondering, "Is this real, or am I dreaming?" I then looked slightly downward to discover the reason the tree line disappeared behind this portion of the wall. It turns out there was a tree line—there was a forest. It's just that it was all growing on the side of a steep mountain. All I could see was the tops of the trees and the forest below. It reminded me of the bus ride—steep drops over large cliffs down the sides of mountains. I inspected the wall a little closer and determined it was built to keep vehicles from going down over this cliff. The wall was maybe five feet thick, about four feet tall, and made from large concrete meshed stones. I wondered why the wall was built so sturdy. Now I knew.

After standing at the wall for a few moments, I decided to continue—start—my jog. Which way to go—left or right? Left would take me back up toward the entrance and past the Mongolian BBQ restaurant I ate dinner at the previous evening. Right would take me up into the woods. A place that looked enchanting, right out of Harry Potter except with an Asian twist. I chose to jog into the enchanted forest.

I weaved through the nicely presented jogging path as it led me past tall trees yet cleared underbrush. It looked like the pristine forest was prepared for a military inspection. Like a team of GIs worked for a week or more tidying up the forest. Again, I was amazed at the attention to detail—the beauty.

I then jogged onto the golf course. Again, it was immaculate. I wasn't a golfer but after looking at the beautiful course, I thought about taking up the sport. For a moment I thought about what it must take to keep the "camp" in such a high presentation state. It didn't take long to get a clue.

I could hear a loud voice off in the distance, so I looked in that direction and saw a line of young men walking across the golf course. About five or ten meters separated them as they formed a human rake—spreading out a hundred yards or so—picking up trash or anything else that didn't belong on the pristine course. The team leader would yell out from time to time directing the operation.

I completed my jog and showered up in my "swanky executive" hotel room and then headed off to do more exploring.

* * *

"What's that?" I asked, pointing to an exotic-looking fruit.

The old woman looked up at me with disbelieving eyes. She was sitting behind a long skinny table full of fresh fruit for sale. I had just come out of the mini-BX (Base Exchange) and saw her set up just outside the back area. I thought it was strange that she set up behind the BX as if she was hiding—too far out of the way. But she had a steady stream of customers. Maybe everyone liked her offerings so much they'd find her setup regardless of how hard she tried to hide.

The lady finished peeling a piece of fruit for another customer and then answered my question, "It's a mango; ever had one before?"

"No."

"It's delicious," she said. "You got to try it."

Originally, I just wanted to know what it was called. Now I was in a negotiation to buy one. She was a good sales lady because I didn't want to get a mango. I simply wanted to know what it was. Her suggestion got me thinking, "Hmm, why wouldn't I try one? Why would I come all the way to the Far East and then only eat stuff I eat back home? No adventure in that."

"Yes, I'll take one please." She picked up a mango and handed it to me. I handed her the money. I paid in US dollars. I forget how much the mango cost, but I do remember being surprised at the low cost of just about everything.

Once the deal was completed, the lady followed up with a question, "Do you want me to cut it for you?" I guess she figured I needed a few clues on how to eat this newfangled fruit I just discovered in my twenty-eighth year of life.

I handed the mango back to her, and she expertly laid it down on the wooden chopping block and started to operate. First she sliced it and a large piece fell to one side. I could see the massive seed in the middle of the part she was still holding. Next, she cut a large piece along the other side of the seed leaving two pieces lying fleshy face up on the cutting board and the third piece, with the large seed, still in her hand. She then peeled the narrow yellow-green skin off the piece she was holding. She gently placed the remaining large seed and surrounding yellow flesh on the wooden cutting board.

The lady created a bit of theatre with the two fleshy pieces. She grabbed one and started cutting parallel lines. Then she turned it ninety degrees and started cutting more parallel lines. The result was a bunch of squares cut into the mango flesh. With both hands she then pushed the skin up into the flesh forming a ready-to-eat—easy to reach—bunch of mango cubes hanging onto the skin by the bottom part of each cube. She repeated this process with the other piece of fleshy mango.

Finally, she put the three ready-to-eat pieces into a paper towel and handed it over to me with an accompanying big smile.

I enjoyed the show. I thanked her and wandered off to look for a place to experience my first mango.

I found a lonely bench in the middle of the enchanted forest and was glad I had an excuse to sit down. After all, I had to eat my mango. It wasn't really my style to just sit down on a public bench and relax. Looking back, I wish it was my style. I wish I did take more time to sit quietly and enjoy nature, take in the scene, contemplate life—think. But my style was more about "looking the part" and "looking cool." I couldn't just sit on bench in the woods by myself—people would think stuff; people would say stuff; can't have that. Sounds dumb, but that's where my head was at.

Glad I had the mango. Now, I could sit down and have an explanation for sitting by myself on a bench up high in the mountains of Benguet Province, Baguio City, Camp John Hay, Philippines. I was ready for anyone passing by, ready to look at them with a reassuring glance that would tell them—without me having to say anything—"Hey, I'm sitting here 'cause I gotta eat my mango. Got a problem with that?" I felt confident as I sat down to enjoy my first mango.

I wasn't really expecting much from my first mango experience. I figured it would be another life let down. "OK, it tastes pretty good but nothing to get excited about. Least I can say I tried it once."

But life has a way of handing out surprises—some good, some bad. I was about to experience one of life's good surprises.

I picked up one piece of mango and looked at the fleshy cubes as they stared back at me. Then I rammed a bunch of them in my mouth and bit down ripping the cubes off the mango skin and onto my tongue. I started to chew the morsels creating a gooey mango pulp. As I chewed, I kept getting shot with heavenly flavor bursts. My taste buds went crazy sending happy signals to my brain. Each signal repeated the same message, "Delicious, delicious, delicious." Followed by "Eat more, eat more, eat more!"

One of my favorite memories of eating my first mango was the sensation of mango juice running down the side of my face. I tried to keep it all contained within my mouth but it was impossible. The juice just sprayed out. I'd never eaten a fruit so fresh, so juicy, and so delicious.

I felt like an ill-mannered schoolboy as I attacked the mango, getting the sticky juice and pulp on my hands and all over my face. But it seemed like that was the best way to eat it; otherwise I would miss out as I watched the juice spill onto the fertile soil below. I didn't want to waste any of it.

I finally finished devouring my first mango. I must have appeared funny-looking as I sat on the bench with my elbows on my knees; hands open and extended still dripping mango juice. Any passing observer could easily tell what I'd done. On the forest floor below, between my legs, sat three items – two inward bent mango skins and a yellow, gnawed at, mango seed - that gave it away. As I looked down at the discarded mango seed it reminded me of Don King the famous boxing promoter who wears his hair sticking straight up. My teeth worked hard trying to extract the delicious flesh from the seed. In doing so, I created a ring of mango fibers sticking straight up in all directions.

As I sat there with mango juice dripping from my fingers, I had only one thought going through my head. The thought had to do with how good the mango tasted. The thought had to do with how I was overwhelmed by this new exotic taste that had just entered my world. The overriding thought was this:

How come it took this long in my life to taste a mango?

I'd missed out all these years. How come I never heard of mango before? How come nobody ever told me about mango?

I sat there on the wooden bench, in the woods, at Camp John Hay, and thought about how great that mango tasted.

I was really starting to believe maybe I had died the night before and gone to heaven.

* * *

I decided to explore Baguio City. So, I simply walked out the Camp John Hay front gate and proceeded to follow "the action." It turns out there was action everywhere. The city started right outside the gate.

I remember seeing and visiting a dry-goods store just to take in the sight. It was very simple. A garage door opened up and goods were on display in a hodgepodge manner, as if they're all going to be sold today anyway so no need to make it all neat. The store owner was very friendly and gave me the impression he knew I wasn't there to buy anything, but he still had no problem with my walking around and taking in the experience.

In a way, I liked the store just the way it was. It came across as real—here's stuff that most people need from day to day and you can buy it. No hard sell, no blue light specials, just a place to go and buy a shovel if you need one. And it seemed devoid of government regulation. Almost like he decided yesterday to start up and— *shazam*—today he's in business. No red tape, no hassles, just do it—make it happen—no show business, no bribes, no government permits and licenses, just start selling stuff.

Next, I wondered off to downtown Baguio. At least it looked like downtown to me. There were market vendors everywhere selling just about everything. I'll bet if I looked hard enough I could have bought the London Bridge. All I had to do was ask, and some guy would have said, "We sold our last one yesterday, but I can reorder another and have it here by tomorrow!"

My shopping attire was deck shoes—no socks—pleated large white shorts, loose fitting short-sleeved shirt, and an important accessory to let everyone know I was from out of town—a Boston Red Sox baseball cap.

I remember walking in the busy city and looking to my right up a steep street. It looked exceptionally busy with vendors strewn along both sides. Most of them set up just off the sidewalk in the street. I had to have a look.

One lady caught my eye. Actually, it wasn't her; it was her offering. Sitting just in front of her were two large white buckets full of a mysterious substance. The substance in one bucket was pinkish and the other brownish. I walked past and stared down into the buckets and wondered to myself, "What's that stuff?"

There was food for sale on both sides of this lady, so I figured it might be some kind of food, but I quickly ruled that out as it didn't look edible. I continued to stare at the Slurpee looking concoction in the two buckets. I'd never seen anything like it before.

My neck almost snapped off as I continued looking backward and downward at the goo in the buckets. Finally, I decided I had to know what it was. I stopped and walked backward to greet the lady, "Hello, can you tell me what's in those buckets?"

The lady sitting on the curb guarding the two big buckets of goo greeted me with a big smile and picked up a large wooden spoon and immediately started stirring the mixture. She then lifted up a gob, and it slobbered off the sides of the spoon and splashed back into the bucket. "Delicious! You like, this one or this one?"

She had a look on her face that spoke to me, "This is the best stuff in town. You don't want to miss out!"

I just wanted to know what it was, but I soon discovered that wasn't going to happen. I was either going to buy some or not. Explanations were not part of the deal.

Later on, when talking to other Filipinos, I discovered what was in the two buckets. It's a Filipino delicacy called *bagoong*—pronounced bah-go-ohng. It's a shrimp paste and a staple *ulam*. "Ulam" is a Filipino word that loosely translates as "something that goes with the rice." You, I, or anyone else can live off rice and bagoong. And apparently, once you acquire the taste for it—it's awesome. Bagoong also goes exceptionally well with green mangos. Green mangos are hard and apparently delicious especially when eaten with bagoong.

After my bagoong experience, I strolled off to Burnham Park. I enjoyed the open area, the green grass, the strategically planted trees, and the sprinkling-water features. Burnham Park is well known. It's a main hangout in Baguio.

While walking the peaceful pathways of Burnham Park, I looked up and noticed I was going to pass by another visitor to the park. Unlike me, this person looked like a special visitor. He came equipped with a sharp-looking blue uniform, a military-style hat, and—for good measure—a sawed-off shotgun.

I wondered, "Hmmm, what's he doing here? Why would a policeman be walking around the park armed with a shotgun? What does that mean? Am I in danger? Is he a real policeman, or could this be trouble? Should I be afraid of him? Should I get off the path and head the other way?"

I didn't want to startle him by suddenly changing direction and darting off. We were too close. If we were further away, I could have made a change of direction look natural. But now it was too late. We would cross paths.

As we closed the distance between us, I could see his face clearly. He had a bit of a scowl, and his eyes were steely. I wondered if he was going to challenge me. After all, "What's a guy doing out here walking around with a sawed-off shotgun? What could he possibly need that for? Is he the park intimidator? Just goes around challenging folks with a show of power?" This was new for me.

Once I could see his face, I knew he could see mine. I wanted to make sure he had no doubts about my friendly intentions. I hit him with the only self-defense weapon at my disposal—I let loose with the biggest smile I could muster! I stretched my lips so they touched both earlobes—I wanted to make sure he saw my smile.

I held my oversized smile for about three paces before I knew it worked. He tried to outdo me, blinding me with his big white teeth showing through his overgrown return smile.

Then I thought about what to say. Just walking past with a jumbo supersized smile seemed ridiculous and unnatural. I wanted to say something to let him know—and to let myself know—that I wasn't afraid. But I had a challenge—what do you say to a guy coming right at you carrying a sawed-off shotgun?

I thought and thought and finally arrived at what I was going to say. I had my speech ready. I waited until we had about two paces separating us; then I delivered my quickly prepared on-the-fly speech, only one word—"Hi!"

I wanted to keep the dialog simple so there'd be no communication mix-up.

His response was pure genius. He said, "Hi!" and continued walking still carrying his sawed-off shotgun and his massive smile.

As we passed, I didn't look back; I just kept walking. After all, I wasn't sure the conversation could get any better—maybe worse, but not better. We smiled, we greeted each other, and then we left—sounds good to me. Besides, what do you talk about with a guy carrying a sawed-off shotgun anyway? "Hey, killed anybody lately?"

I thought it was very odd to see the shotgun-man in the park. It seemed like such a contrast. Here we have a restful, peaceful, and beautiful park. Now let's add an accessory, something every park needs to enhance the experience—a uniformed guy walking around with a sawed-off shotgun.

The shotgun man didn't fit the scene. To me it felt so out of place, like attending a formal wedding reception at an elegant seaside mansion where everyone is dressed in tuxedos and you bump into a guy wearing boxer shorts. It's ridiculous and inappropriate—not the "done thing."

Well, by the end of the day, my opinion changed. I noticed the shotgun man appearing in more and more places. Not sure why I never noticed him—I mean them—before. I saw him in front of every bank entrance, most restaurants, and randomly on street corners. Same uniform, same sawed-off shotgun. Apparently, Mr. Shotgun was just another part of the landscape, and everyone seemed to accept his presence—no big deal; that's how we roll here. For me it was all new. I wasn't used to seeing such a brazen show of firepower out in the public like that. I was used to it on the air-force base but not out in the public areas. Almost felt like the whole town was an extension of the military base—complete with guards and all.

* * *

"Welcome home to Clark Air Base, the largest US overseas military installation in the world," declared the bus driver as we drove through the gate. I accepted his boast, but I'll bet there are some folks who would challenge that claim.

After two nights away on a Baguio adventure, we arrived back on base. I slept for most of the trip to avoid getting frightened by the treacherous drive.

A cheering group of kids lined the side of the road outside the gate to greet us. They were hooping, hollering, and jumping up and down like we were going to start handing out hundred dollar bills.

As I looked at these young children I wondered, "How can they be so happy?" Most of them were exceptionally skinny and wore ragged clothes. Since there were so many of them and so few adults, I wondered if maybe they were homeless; maybe they had no parents. I immediately scratched that thought from my mind. I didn't want to think about it. I didn't want to know.

Finally, the bus stopped in front of Kelly Cafeteria, and we all got out. As I stood waiting for my luggage, Rosita called out, "Remember to give me a call, Sean. I'll send my nephew to pick you up and bring you by the house for a visit."

12. ANGELES CITY

I waited outside the main gate for Rosita's nephew Manuel to pick me up. I'd arranged the pickup with Rosita, calling her from the hallway wall phone back at the barracks. She was glad to hear from me and quickly dispatched Manuel. Rosita was following through on her invitation for me to come over, meet the family, and enjoy some home-cooked Filipino food. I was excited about the prospects. I felt honored to be invited. I was looking forward to the adventure.

Only one problem: I'd never seen Rosita's nephew Manuel before. And Manuel had never seen me. As the agreed meeting time crept ever more into the past, I began to wonder if I was destined for another unexciting meal by myself on base. Rosita told me to be on the lookout for a jeep. That's like telling someone in New York City to be on the lookout for yellow cab—they're everywhere! She told me he'd be able to pick me out, so I shouldn't worry, just be waiting outside the main gate in the visitors area. So, I waited.

Of the many jeeps in the area, one caught my eye. It pulled up about twenty-five yards away. The driver and his three passengers climbed out and looked at me. I looked back and wondered, "Could that be Manuel?" The driver started walking toward me. Well, truth is, he hobbled over. He had a serious limp. His right leg remained straight as his left leg carried out most of the work involved in walking. He leaned while he walked. He sported a wide-eyed smile. He called out from ten or so paces away, "Hello, Sean!"

I walked over to greet him, "Manuel?" We shook hands, turned, and walked back to the jeep. His three passengers stared at me all wearing the same expression—big smiles. They looked like the welcoming crew on the "Love Boat." I was immediately drawn to them.

Manuel and his companions greeted me like I was a long-lost friend, like we'd all gone to grade school together. I cheerfully— and without reservation—hopped into the waiting jeep and we drove off into the unknown of Angeles City.

They could have taken me anywhere. I was fresh meat. But I didn't have a negative thought in any part of my brain. I was off to visit Rosita and her Filipino family. I was in good hands. Manuel and his friends were my guardians. They would make sure I arrived safely and without incident.

And that's exactly what happened.

Looking back I have to wonder if I should have been a bit more cautious before taking off with a carload of strangers in Angeles City. But I remember not being concerned at all. I was all trusting.

I felt like a VIP as they insisted I get in the front passenger seat while Manuel's three friends squeezed into the back. Manuel took on the driving duties.

I listened with amazement as they launched into an animated conversation in Filipino. I enjoyed watching them converse. They appeared more confident talking in their own language. The vocal sounds fascinated me. I wondered how they could be intelligible, how they made sense, how they could be a means of communication. But they were.

When they talked with me, I could almost feel the translation delay—think it in Filipino first, then internally translate to English, and finally speak it. The translation delay was virtually unnoticeable—their English was fantastic. It's just that listening to them speak Filipino I could sense the difference. When speaking Filipino they were on home turf; they were in their element. English, on the other hand, would slow them down, not allow them to express their thoughts as easily or as eloquently. I admired the fact that they spoke multiple languages. This was another case—among many—where I felt inadequate because I spoke only one language. Once again, I was "Mr. One-Talk."

As I studied and analyzed the lively body language and vocal expressions, I was fairly confident I knew what they were talking about. During a pause, I checked to see if I was correct by asking Manuel, "Are you talking about the best way to get to the house?"

"Yes. Gil wants to take a shortcut, but I think it's better to stick to the main roads," replied Manuel. "Either way will be fine, but I'm going to keep to the main road."

"Are you stationed at Clark?" Manuel asked.

I gave my standard reply, "No, just here visiting. I'm stationed in Colorado..."

The jeep stopped in front of a concrete wall about my height—six feet. On top of the wall was a short fence made of steel rods with pointy tips. Then all along the topside of the concrete wall was a sprinkling of broken glass. It was a formidable defensive perimeter.

One of the Manuel's friends hopped out of the back, opened the locked gate, and we majestically drove onto the compound. I watched as he closed the gate leaving us securely inside the fortified area. I felt like I was in a James Bond movie entering the secret headquarters reserved only for special agents. I wasn't used to a neighborhood house having this much security. I wondered why.

The front door opened, and there stood Rosita. "Sean, glad you could make it. Hope you're hungry because we've got lots of food."

Even though I trusted Manuel and his friends, I was relieved to see Rosita and hear her voice. Now, I had concrete proof I was at the right house. I really started to relax about my situation. I felt more at ease and comfortable. Yes, the security situation was a bit "over-the-top"—like a mini-Fort Knocks—but it was still a warm and welcoming environment.

I was offered one of the fancy chairs in the living room area and started scanning my surroundings. There was a lot to see. The room was very busy with furniture, wall hangings and knick-knacks. One prominent wall hanging was a huge wooden framed picture of President Kennedy—JFK. Another was an even larger framed picture of Jesus. And I couldn't help noticing a giant wooden spoon and fork set hanging off another wall. In between all these giant wall ornaments were smaller ones. It seemed like the interior decorator was playing a game—fill up every open wall space with some kind of trinket. It made for eye-catching scenery.

Behind my chair was a raised landing with a railing. Stairs at both ends made for easy access to this open hallway. Along the open hallway were three doors, which I assumed were the bedrooms. I never looked into the kitchen, but I could see the opening and smell the aroma of exotic foods being prepared. The smell was divine. I was looking forward to a home-cooked meal.

Rosita introduced me to everyone. There was Rosita's Mom and Dad, her sister, her niece Tin-Tin, whom I met on the bus to Baguio, and her nephew Manuel. And a whole host of other relatives who came by to see Rosita on her visit back to the Philippines from California. Manuel's friends stuck around to enjoy the festivities as well.

Rosita's Dad sat across from me in what looked like the most elegant chair in the home. He kicked off the conversation asking, "So, how do you like the Philippines?"

"I like it; very nice. People are very friendly."

"Tell me something: do Americans think Filipinos have tails? Do they think we're monkeys?"

Rosita spoke up, "Daddy, stop it!"

Her Dad was having no part of it. He had an American in the house. He was going to ask the questions—any questions he wanted.

"I've heard Americans think Filipinos have tails, that we're related to the monkeys; I just wanted to find out if it's true. Is it? Do Americans think Filipinos are monkeys?"

"No, sir. Never heard that before," I stammered.

"Well, that's good to know. I remember coming back to the Philippines from Japan after the war and being treated like a second-class citizen in my own country. And you know who treated me like that?"

"No, sir."

"The Americans—young, wet-behind-the-ears privates ordering me around. When I got off the plane, they directed me to go in the line for Filipinos where we were subjected to all kinds of scrutiny while the Americans were sent on through with no checks, no waiting—the VIP treatment. I resented that; I still resent it.

"Can you imagine that happening in your own country? Can you imagine coming home from the war and going to the United States and seeing Filipino soldiers treated like VIPs and American soldiers like second-class citizens? How would you feel?"

His story and follow up rhetorical questions hit me with the same effect as a swinging baseball bat to the face. I felt pain with a good helping of embarrassment and wondered if I should've stayed on base where it's safer—less chance of encountering uncomfortable questioning. But at the same time I was taking it all in. I was learning something. This is how you find out the history books are not always accurate; many are missing a critical ingredient, a critical aspect, a critical and usually overlooked element—*the truth!*

The truth can be inconvenient; it can ruin a good story; it can turn a good guy into a bad guy in an instant. As an American, I thought I was a good guy, but I was getting a history lesson painting "Mr. America" as maybe not as nice as I thought; not as nice as the history books told me.

I paused to collect my thoughts, but then got saved by the bell—the dinner bell. Rosita yelled, "Kain na Tayo!" (Let's eat!)

I didn't have to move. I was handed a plate full of delicious smelling but exotic-looking food. The room went quiet as everyone starting digging in.

Resting on my plate were two small spring rolls, a pile of skinny noodles, and another pile of white rice.

"I gave you a sample, Sean. That's *lumpia* (as she pointed to the spring rolls); that's *pansit* (as her finger moved, now pointing to the noodles); and of course that's rice. Help yourself to more and all the other foods. Save room for desert!" explained Rosita.

Just as I finished my second plate of food, Tin-Tin came by with a tiny banana and dropped it on my plate: "This is what we have for desert."

The tiny banana tasted great, much better than the big bananas I was used to from back home. I wonder if the taste difference was mainly due to freshness. These little bananas were probably grown just outside the house and picked that morning. The big bananas I ate back home were probably grown overseas and spent days or weeks in a frozen shipping container. It's hard to complete with fresh.

The conversation became colorful, cordial, and interesting. Rosita's Dad had broken the ice. His line of questioning opened up the air, brought about a feeling of honesty, as if we could discuss just about anything. I felt comfortable enough to bring up something I'd heard about; something very popular in the Philippines but illegal in the United States.

"Can you tell my about the cockfights?" I asked rather brazenly.

Manuel responded, "Have you ever been?"

"No."

"Want to go? We can take you this Sunday. I'll pick you up at the base—same place we picked you up today."

I quickly agreed to this offer. I was booked in. I was excited.

Then Manuel made another offer.

"Sean, want to go out with us tonight? We're going to our favorite club; want to join us?

"Yeah, love to," I replied automatically.

I was getting into the thick of it. I was doing what I set out to do, discover the Philippines. Mix in. Get involved.

That evening...

"Sean, this song is for you. Listen carefully; I'm singing this just for you," said Carlo as he got up from our table and walked to the back end of the club. He entered a booth, picked up the microphone, and gave a short intro speech to the entire audience, "This song is for my friend Sean." He added effect by pointing his finger toward me. I could feel the gaze of the entire audience as they looked to see who this "Sean" guy was.

The club was unique. It was half inside and half outside. We were sitting in the transition area—half our table was inside; half outside. If I looked straight up, I could see the edge of the roof. If I looked straight down, I could see where the club floor went from concrete to dirt. The club spilled out onto the street. Tables and chairs spread out on the dirt area directly outside the club. It wasn't fancy but it was welcoming.

The music started. Carlo began singing, and I began slouching down in my chair. I'm glad it was relatively dark so no-one could see the red embarrassment line rising up my neck and face.

"I love you! You are my love!" Carlo belted out at max volume. "I will always be with you; never ever going to leave you; you are my forever love..."

I looked around the club searching for reactions. I was amazed. Folks were behaving as if everything was ... normal! They had confident smiles on their faces as if all the world's problems were suddenly gone; nothing to worry about—life is good.

I, on the other hand, felt extremely awkward thinking, "I'm in a night club in Angeles City with a group of Filipinos I just met a few hours ago, and one of them has a microphone and a large captive audience and is singing me a love song! Nothing strange here, perfectly normal!"

I tried to carry a confident smile as I scanned the room. But my confidence took another hit as Manuel placed his hand on my leg and asked me, "Isn't it a great song? Do you like it?"

I smiled and nodded a disbelieving "Yes." Then I thought, "Why is he putting his hand on my leg? What's going on here? Is this OK? It doesn't seem OK." Having another man put his hand on my leg was outside my experience. I was not tolerating it—emotionally—very well.

I did my best to remain calm as "Carlo the Crooner" serenaded me while Manuel rested one hand on my leg and wrapped the other around my shoulder. I didn't panic. I considered it. But I ruled it out quickly. I figured there wasn't much I could do anyway, so just go with it. "I'm not in any danger, nothing life threatening going on. Hey, here's an idea—maybe I should just *relax*!"

That's when I began to observe my surroundings more carefully and noticed—once again—I was the only uncomfortable person. Everyone else seemed to be enjoying themselves and not at all concerned about Carlo singing me a love song. I also noticed men putting their hands on other men's legs and wrapping their arms around each other's shoulders—no big deal. It appeared this was not unusual; it appeared to be ... normal.

Once I worked out that everything was "chill," I lost my red face and began to relax and enjoy the experience. I wasn't bothered by Manuel putting his hand on my leg or when he put his arm around my shoulder. I felt accepted, like he was welcoming me into their inner circle.

When Carlo finished "crooning," he looked the audience straight in the eye, opened his arms wide, and announced, "That was for my new friend Sean!" The crowd erupted with cheers. I was proud of myself as I stood up, smiled, and waved. I wasn't even embarrassed. I overcame my anxiety about all the affection and love bouncing around club. I wasn't used to it. Maybe it was the beer kicking in or maybe it was something I couldn't resist—maybe no one can resist it—the feeling of being accepted. I liked it.

Carlo made his way back to our table, the crowd cheering him all the way. I gave him a "high five" and bought another round of San Miguel beer.

After our evening of laughing, crooning, and beer drinking, Manuel drove me back to the base. During the trip he told me how he got his limp.

"I was down in Manila going to school and found myself in the middle of a protest. Someone tossed a hand grenade. I got it. But I was lucky. Two people died; I just ended up in the hospital for a month, and now I only have this limp. I came out all right. I could have ended up dead. A limp sure beats death!"

I listened and tried to fathom being in the middle of a protest where people are throwing hand grenades.

We pulled up to the main gate, and I got out of the jeep. I thanked Manuel and his friends for a great evening. I felt like I'd been shown an inside glimpse of the "Filipino way." By hanging out with only Filipinos, I got a chance to see how they operate, how they think, how they act … how they roll.

As I walked up to the gate to show my ID card, a lady started talking rapidly and moved closer to me. I didn't understand a word and didn't think much of it until the Filipino gate guard asked me, "Is this your wife?"

"No."

"She's telling us she's your wife. She says you're acting like you don't know her, but she's your wife. Is she your wife?"

"No. I don't know her," I replied.

"OK, sir. We'll take care of it."

I walked past the guard through the gate and could hear the lady yelling louder as she passionately pleaded her case. But it didn't work. The guards wouldn't let her on base.

Something told me this was not a unique occurrence.

13. COCKFIGHTS

I watched like a spellbound schoolboy dazzled by a magician. One man held the rooster's legs facing outward as he pressed the body of the bird between his arms and against his belly. Another man worked diligently tying a curved long razorblade to the bird's leg. The man doing the holding gazed upon the man tying up the razorblade like a father watching his son get stitched up by a doctor. The razorblade man was an expert, a guru, a master. He worked with an air of competence, and everyone standing around watching remained silent as we observed the master demonstrate his skill.

There was no signal between the master and the man holding the bird to indicate the procedure had finished. The man holding the bird simply walked away. He had a knowing smile, appearing to be a happy customer. The master never looked up.

The next man in line stood before the razorblade doctor, and the whole procedure started again. I saw a line of men holding roosters waiting—in assembly-line fashion—to be treated by the razorblade doctor.

Manuel followed up on his promise to take me to the cockfights. Now I was there walking through the gathering crowds and witnessing the prefight activities. Manuel, Carlo, Gil, Ares, and I would make the Cockpit Arena our hangout for the next several hours or so. I entered a new world—a world previously unknown to me.

I was excited. I'd heard about the cockfights; now I was going to witness it firsthand. And I was there with the locals, the best way to travel. I don't think I ever would have ventured to such an event on my own or with a bunch of Americans from the base.

I was taking it all in. As the five of us stood about half way up the bleachers, I focused on capturing a detailed mental image. The stadium was a combination of metal and wood. It looked like it was built mainly for function not for show, nothing fancy, just the necessities. The audience bleachers surrounded the cockfighting area. The bleachers had a foot rest and a place to sit but were otherwise open. I could see all the way to the ground below. The cockfighting ring looked about the same size as a boxing ring. The fence around the ring had two levels. The bottom level was some sort of a clear Plexiglas, the top a metal fence with vertically spaced bars similar to what you'd have around your swimming pool. The spaced bars were close enough together to prevent the roosters from getting out, but far enough apart so spectators could see into the ring.

The bleachers were about half filled to capacity. That's still a lot of people. I'd estimate there were at least a thousand spectators. And these folks were noise makers. They were not shy about cranking up the volume level. As I watched the cockfighting scene unfold, I noticed a repeating pattern.

First, the contestants would bring out their roosters and show them off to the audience to get the betting started. In one corner of the ring was a sign hanging down from the roof with the word "Wala." In the other corner, a sign with the word "Mayroon." Each contestant, holding their rooster, stood under one of the signs. Bets were then placed on either the Wala bird or the Mayroon bird.

By the way, *wala* is Tagalog for "I don't have" or "nothing." *mayroon* translates roughly as "I do have" or "something." Not sure why they use these conventions but I'm just the reporter— that's what I observed.

The betting ritual is crazy. Everyone knew when to start. There didn't seem to be anyone directing anything. It all just happened.

Hands flew up in the air followed by yelling. The yelling only involved two words—either "wala" or "mayroon." A person yelling "wala" would lock eyes with someone yelling "mayroon" and agree on a betting amount. That sealed the deal. Once you lock eyes and agree on the amount, you're under contract. Done—not getting out of it; you own it.

I hope you're asking the question, "But how did they agree on the price?" After all, the only words used were "wala" and "mayroon," and that doesn't tell you the amount of the bet. Well, it turns out the amount is all done visually. It's done by hand—put your hand up, and place your bet with your fingers. Fingers pointing up are the higher bets; fingers down are lower denominations. The spectators had it hard wired. They had no trouble placing bets.

I also noticed many spectators placing multiple bets. I struggled to understand how they could keep track of it all. But when a fight ended, I got to see the payout process in action—money thrown everywhere around the stadium! The losers would roll up paper pesos and throw it to the winners. I watched in astonishment as people carried out this payment procedure in a timely, orderly, and relatively pleasant manner. I couldn't get over watching people pay their unsecured bad debts so willingly. I figured there'd be a few dodgy characters causing a stir, not wanting to pay. I expected fights to break out in the stands. But it never happened. All I witnessed was the orderly—and almost cordial—exchange of money between betters.

I got a lesson in betting etiquette when I decided to scratch my nose. As soon as my index finger touched the itchy part of my nose, my hand got pulled down. This corrective action was followed by a respectful but firm admonishment.

"Are you placing a bet for five hundred pesos?" Manual yelled so he could be heard over all the yelling.

"No!" I yelled back.

"Then you want to keep your hands down during the betting. If some guy in here thinks you bet five hundred, you'll have to pay if your bird loses. Always keep your hands down when the betting starts, unless you want to place a bet, OK?"

I quickly shoved my hands in my pockets. I wasn't ready to enter the cockpit betting world just yet.

As I stood there witnessing the wild betting going on around me— hands securely in my pockets—I started wondering. I had a question. I wanted to clarify something. What held it all together?

What made everyone behave so orderly? What compelled people to pay up after placing a losing bet?

With my hands still lodged deep in my pockets, I turned to Manuel and asked, "What if I placed a bet for five hundred pesos, and I only had hundred pesos in my pocket? If my bird lost—what would happen?"

I waited patiently for an answer, but all I got was a blank stare. Then I watched as Manuel turned to his friends and started an animated discussion.

After their short twenty-second discussion, Manuel turned to me and said, "Sean, I'll have to think about that one."

I let it go figuring maybe it's a question you're not supposed to ask. Was I breaching etiquette again? I didn't know. But the answer may just explain why everyone is so well behaved. What's the glue that holds this whole operation together, makes it work, keeps it from turning into a war zone?

Fifteen or twenty minutes later—long after I'd forgotten the question—Manuel, suddenly spoke up. "I've got the answer to your question. We've been talking about it, and now we know what would happen."

"Great, so tell me. If I couldn't cover my five-hundred-peso bet, what would happen?"

He gave me an answer I never expected. I thought he'd tell me something like, "You'll have to go to the bank and make

120

arrangement to pay" or "You could make installment payments" or some other easygoing way to solve the problem.

But that's not what he told me. Instead, he told me the truth, the reality, the facts. And I appreciated it, although I didn't like it. I found out they play for keeps in Angeles City. *This ain't no nursery school. This ain't no place to be if you ain't tough. This ain't no place for sissies. This ain't no place for little boys.*

Here's the answer—here's what Manuel told me.

"You'd never make it out of here alive!"

He continued, "See the four exit doors? They have guards posted. There's no way you can get out of here if you owe money. They'll get you; you'll pay, or you'll die. We never thought about it because you just don't do that. It's something nobody would ever think of doing because you'd be dead. It's not worth dying over."

As Manuel explained, I pushed my hands deeper into my pockets. I wasn't risking it.

I closely observed the brutal sport. Each cockfight usually ended with one bird dead, sometimes both. In the case of both birds dying, the winner just lived a little longer, while the loser was killed instantly. The massive blade on the bird's leg made sure of that. One swipe to the vital organs and lights out, game over, or—as they say in Tagalog, *tapos na*, which means "finished."

I didn't enjoy watching the birds get killed. But I wasn't there to judge the event; I was there to observe. And I observed the way the owners treated their birds. They seemed to have a special caring for the birds both before and after a fight. After the cockfight, the winning rooster is treated as a conquering hero; the losing rooster as an injured family member rushed off to receive medical treatment in a bid to save the bird if possible. I could see the pain in the owner's eyes when his bird lost. And for me this was puzzling— then why put him in the ring? But I was there to observe, not judge.

* * *

As we left the stadium to go home, I noticed someone, a familiar face, a person I'd met on the streets of Angeles City. Now he was sitting outside the cockfight stadium. I witnessed the mad rush of people around him. They were calling out orders, and he filled them with the speed, accuracy, and efficiency of a seasoned baseball park peanut vendor. He handed or tossed over the product with one hand and collected the money with the other. He would organize the change as he swung around and grabbed another product for the next customer. He reminded me of the Tasmanian devil cartoon character—a swirling dust storm—yet controlled like a smoothly operating gearbox.

I felt compelled to talk to him. I had to say hello. I was astonished at the transformation. He had gone through a metamorphosis— changed from a panhandler to a businessman. Somehow I'd recognized the potential when I first met him, but now he was showing it in all its glory; he was demonstrating his talent, his knack for gainful enterprise. I was impressed. I was moved. I almost wanted to ask him for an autograph.

The familiar face, the budding businessman was none other than my dear old street panhandler, Billy Bong.

As I got closer to the scene, I saw the product ... what Billy was selling. He made a smart choice, a fast seller, a product in extremely high demand—cigarettes. I only had to wait about five minutes before he sold out. His selling area quickly became deserted, and that's when I went over to greet him, "BB, how are ya?"

"Hello, Joe! I don't have any more cigarettes, sold out. Sorry." He didn't know my name, so he called me Joe, which is the name given to most foreigners from the West. Joe is short for GI Joe.

"That's OK. I just wanted to congratulate you on your business. What a great idea—selling cigarettes."

"Thanks, Joe."

"My name's Sean by the way. Call me Sean, OK?"

"OK, Mr. Sean."

"This is a great location. The crowd was huge. How long have you been here?" I inquired.

"Got here early this morning, took a jeepney, and been selling all day. I'd sell even more, but I could only carry so much. I carried four bags full of cigarettes, but I still sold out. It's a great business."

"So, you just gonna sell on Sundays at the cockfights?"

"Oh no, I'll be selling outside the main gate at the base. I got a place all picked out. I'll be there every day, starting tomorrow."

"That's great. So you'll be selling every day—making a nice income."

"Yes, sir," he said accompanied with a big businessman grin. "Hey Mr. Sean, would you do me a favor? Would you tell the other GIs about my business? Tell them to buy their cigarettes from me?"

I was sold—I would tell everyone and anyone. I became a member of the BB fan club.

14. MASTER SALESMAN

I watched in amazement as Billy Bong demonstrated master salesmanship skills. The cigarettes flew from his hands into the hands of customers looking to fill their lungs up with smoke. I figured the smoggy and smoky Angeles City air would be sufficient, but these customers wanted more—more smoke for the lungs. Billy Bong wasn't in the business of providing what these people needed. Instead—in the interest of making money and hence making a living—he provided what they wanted. They wanted cigarettes; he sold them cigarettes.

I watched as the cash flowed in one direction. Like the flow of a mighty river in one direction to the sea, the flow of cash moved in one direction—from the customer's pocket into Billy Bong's pocket.

I was checking out Billy Bong's new location outside the main gate. His setup was basic. And I mean basic. No big store front. No Walmart greeters. No big parking lot...just him, his cigarettes, and the street. No protection from the sun. No protection from the rain. No protection from the dangerous streets of Angeles City, just Billy Bong against the world. And from where I was standing, it looked like Billy Bong was winning!

He parked himself on the sidewalk a couple of hundred yards from the main gate and started selling. No big fanfare, no big neon sign, no bells ringing, just BB selling cigarettes and customers lined up to buy them.

He had a permanent smile on his face. His customers were smiling. Everyone seemed to be winning. I wanted to know his secret. I talked to a few happy customers.

"How come everyone wants to buy cigarettes from BB?"

"He's got the lowest prices, and we all like him. Everybody knows BB; he's the best and—did I mention—he's got the lowest priced cigarettes in the city. No one can beat his price."

"Yeah, BB's the best. Everybody looks out for him. We keep an eye out to make sure he's OK. He's safe as long as he's in Angeles."

I was puzzled by the last statement. "He's safe...what does he mean by that? Why would BB not be safe?" I found it strange.

I hung around until BB sold all his cigarettes. I wanted to help him. I wanted to see him succeed. I was drawn by his ambition.

"Hi, BB. Good work selling them cigarettes. Are you going to get more?"

"Hi, Mr. Sean. You bet. I'll get another supply early tomorrow morning. I can only carry so many boxes. Maybe later I'll get a wagon or something to carry them in so I can get more each day. But for now, I'll just bring what I can carry."

He continued with his business lecture, "Tomorrow, I'm gonna start selling more products. I've got enough money to buy more supplies. So, I'm gonna make even more money tomorrow, you'll see."

"What other products?

"You'll see. I'm definitely gonna get some rice, coffee, and sugar. Those are the biggest sellers. Oh, and I want to get *balut* too—people love that stuff, especially for *merienda*."

Balut is the duck egg I learned about on my trip to Baguio. I found out "merienda" means "break time." Apparently, balut is a favorite with construction workers when they're taking a break in the afternoon; it gives them renewed energy.

I thought about BB's setup—a little too basic for my taste. I wasn't criticizing him; I just wanted to contribute to his business, and I came up with a way to do it.

"BB, have you thought about setting up a stall? Like the other ones around here?"

The street was lined with stalls. Just stick pole frames with different colored tarps. Nothing fancy but they seemed to be the rage. These simple stalls were functional. At least it would get BB out of the hot sun, and give him a bit of business privacy.

"Great idea, but I don't have money for that. Right now I need to sell and make more money; then later I can set up a stall."

I had my chance. I took it. "What if I get it for you? What do you need?"

"Really? A stall? For me?"

"Yeah, c'mon; let's go shopping."

BB and I walked to a couple of shops nearby and started gathering the gear. I was dazzled by this kid's street smarts. He did all the negotiating. He'd haggle the salesman down to the lowest price, and then I paid the bill. I paid in pesos. Converting to US dollars, I spent maybe a total of twenty-five bucks to get everything. The best twenty-five dollars I ever spent.

We put the finishing touches on the new stall and then stood back to gaze upon the glorious structure. Turns out it was easier to construct than I thought. BB's stall was just an extension off the row of stalls already on the streets. By doing this, we already had one wall. Then we built a simple frame from bamboo and used three tarps to cover the top, back, and remaining side. A table and chair sat in the front with another tarp to close off the front at nighttime, nothing fancy but very functional. BB stared at the finished product and beamed with pride. I beamed too. I felt good.

As we were setting up the new stall, I noticed a small baby lying on the sidewalk sandwiched between two small pieces of cardboard. The most important piece of cardboard was the top one; otherwise the poor kid would have burned up in the sun. I watched and wondered why no one seemed to be taking responsibility. I blew it off, figuring the mother was nearby somewhere. There were a lot of people around, and nobody took any notice. So I just followed their lead and ignored the seemingly abandoned baby.

"OK, BB. I'm heading back to the base; I'll see you tomorrow."

"Thank you very much, Mr. Sean. I love my new stall. It's the best!"

At that moment something came over me. Something told me to ask BB just one more question. For some reason I wanted to know if he was going to be all right. I'm not sure why, but I had to ask.

"BB, do you need a ride home? I'll get you a cab."

I wasn't ready for his answer. I'm still not even ready to write it down as I type away at this book. It's called reality. BB was about to invite me into his reality—his "in your face" reality.

"I don't need a ride 'cause I don't have a home. I've been living on the streets for the past two years. I'll be staying right here in my new stall. This is the best home I've ever had in my life. This is even better than the home we had in Manila."

I cringed. I sunk low. I flopped. I mentally collapsed. I wasn't ready for reality. I wish I hadn't asked. I wish I didn't know. Then I could go on living in my fantasy world where everybody has a nice home and everybody's happy. I wasn't in that world anymore.

Reality—my hero businessman BB lived on the streets of Angeles City and had been doing so for the past two years! And I scolded him a week ago for begging! I felt like becoming a beggar—I wanted to beg him for forgiveness.

"You don't have a home?" I asked in a disbelieving voice.

"Yeah. I told you, I live on the streets. I've been doing it a long time; I'm good at it. No problem. Lots of kids live on the streets. I'm not the only one. It's no big deal; we're used to it."

I couldn't take it anymore. "BB, you want to stay on base with me? Or can I get you a hotel room?"

"No way, I'm staying right here. This is my new home, and I don't want anyone to take it. If I leave it and come back, someone will be in it. No way, I'm staying right here. Besides, this place is nice. I'm not used to something this fancy."

"Are you sure?" I attempted to talk him out of it. At this point my motivation was to ease my mind; BB was fine. He wanted no part of my offer. I felt like I was talking to an adult. Someone who knew what he was doing and didn't need my help. He didn't need anyone's help. He could make it on his own.

"Listen, Mr. Sean, I'm staying right here. I can't go. I won't go. I must stay here. Don't worry, I'll be fine. This place is way better and way safer than what I'm used to."

Even though he was adamant about staying in his brand-new street stall, I was still puzzled by his stubbornness. I felt as if he wasn't telling me something, as if there was more to the story. And I guess I was glad. I wasn't ready for anymore truth. I could barely digest the truth bomb he already dropped on me. Now I knew...my young-hero entrepreneur was homeless—he lived on the streets of Angeles City.

I said good-bye, turned, and started walking toward the main gate. I looked back at BB and his new stall to verify it wasn't a dream, to verify I wasn't hallucinating, to verify it was real, to verify I wasn't waking up from a nightmare. It was much worse than a nightmare—it was "in-your-face" reality.

I felt like a loser leaving BB on the street. It would have been easy if I didn't know the truth, but I knew. I walked away anyway. I went back to my comfortable barracks. My so-called crappy barracks was like a five-star Las Vegas hotel compared to BB's market stall. I was having a difficult time dealing with my new reality.

15. SPECIAL DEAL

What's wrong, Sean?" asked Antonio, at our "back of the barracks" gathering. There was a group of us scattered, some sitting on the recently mowed green grass, some on the concrete ramp, some on empty milk crates, and some standing around. It was about 4:30 p.m., and I offered to buy some beer, so the workers stuck around knocking down a few cold San Miguels.

I looked up at Antonio and stated flatly, "I helped this kid set up a market stall today. He's a business wizard. I really like him. Then I find out he lives on the street—got no home. I'm devastated. I feel so guilty hanging out enjoying a beer, living on base in the barracks while he's living on the street."

Antonio tried to make me feel better. "Don't worry about it. Those street kids can handle themselves. Besides, nothing you can do; there so many of them. At least you helped one."

"The kid is good," I continued. "He can sell like nobody's business, sells out all his cigarettes by noon. They say he's got the lowest prices and the best cigarettes."

"Are you talking about BB—Billy Bong?" yelled out someone in the group.

My eyes lit up; I was surprised. "Yeah, how'd you know?"

"C'mon, everybody knows BB. He's the most popular kid on the street. The GIs love him. They look out for him. We all love him. He's also popular with the bosses, and that's how he got the special cigarette deal."

Antonio could see the confused look on my face, so he started giving me the low down. "Sean, you better be careful hanging out with BB. I know you're trying to be a nice guy, but you better be careful. BB's popular with everyone, even the bosses. And the bosses are a rough bunch."

"The bosses? What are you talking about?"

"Where do you think BB got his cigarettes from? Did he tell you? Did you ask him? If you knew, I bet you wouldn't be hanging out with him."

"I don't get it. What are you talking about? What do you mean, where did he get the cigarettes from?"

"BB's got a special deal, one of a kind. I'm not sure if I should tell you 'cause it may just get you in trouble. 'Course if you're hanging out with BB—helping him set up a stall—you're probably already in trouble. So, I might just as well tell you."

I stared at Antonio, not sure if I wanted to know. I had enough truth for one day; I didn't know if I could stand up to any more.

"Sean, BB is selling stolen cigarettes. Everyone knows it. But no one will ever say anything—not good for your health, if you get what I mean."

I mentally slapped my forehead as I thought back to the base newspaper article about the stolen cigarettes. "No, not BB!" I started to really hate the truth. I was having a hard time handling it. Reality was becoming my enemy.

Antonio continued, "The local bosses recruited BB to steal the cigarettes. They taught him how to open the crates coming in from Subic. He can open the seal and then put it back and no one can tell, no one can tell it was tampered with. He does it with only a piece of metal wire and his bare hands. They say it takes him less than three minutes. Then he offloads the cigarette cases to a waiting jeepney. They pay BB with cartons of cigarettes, which he sells on the streets. It's ingenious. Wish I'd thought of it."

"How come they got a little kid doing the dirty work?" I asked like a real out-of-towner, like a guy with no street smarts, like a guy who just got off the turnip truck.

"That's just it. They figure, if BB gets caught, nothing will happen. He's just a kid. And BB knows not to snitch. That's a life-threatening activity. Snitching is something you do only one time—after that, you're dead."

"Why are you telling me all this, Antonio? Aren't you afraid I'll run off and tell the base commander? He's looking to catch these guys—even got a big reward out for info on who did it?

My naïve and goofy questions brought forth heavy laughter. I was out of my league.

Antonio squared me away, "Why am I telling you this? Let's see ... I want you to live! The bosses see you snooping around BB's operation, and they might get suspicious. Chances are they won't care 'cause even if you turn them in, nothing will happen, but you never know. I'm telling you more as a warning. You may be getting in over your head. Even though you're trying to help out a street kid, it could get you in big trouble."

I started getting nervous. My response was to ask more questions, dig myself in deeper and deeper, "So, you don't care if I run off and report this to the base commander?"

"Doesn't bother me a bit, but it's not a good move, hombre. Who's going to believe you? They won't be able to find any witnesses to corroborate your story. No one will talk. You'll end up looking foolish and making lots of enemies; I'd highly recommend against it."

I kept digging, "How 'bout if I told the local police?"

That question really got a belly laugh.

"The police? You kiddin'? The police are all on the payroll; bosses got them bought and paid for."

Antonio continued to enlighten me.

"And no GIs can arrest BB either. Angeles City is outside US jurisdiction, so they can't touch him. The commander has to work through the local authorities, and they'll never cooperate; they'll never bring in BB or any of the bosses. So, if you want to report it to the base commander, go ahead, be my guest.

"Besides, I thought you said you liked BB? And you're going to turn him in?"

He called me out. He called my bluff. He was asking me if I would turn in a homeless street kid trying to make a living. Am I that cruel? Am I that much of a traitor?

I quickly replied, "Nah, I'm not gonna say anything. I would never do anything to get BB in trouble. I'm just trying to find out what's going on, how this all works. I want BB to do well. I just wish he wasn't selling stolen cigarettes."

Antonio schooled me on street reality. "What else is the kid gonna do? The bosses ask him to be part of the deal, and what's he gonna say—'no'? Forget it. He's a smart kid; they recognize that, and that's why they brought him in on the team. Besides, the kid's gotta make a living; what do you want him to do—starve? He's begging on the streets, and beggars don't make that much. You should be happy for him, be glad he's got this good gig."

I listened with the concentration of a paratrooper getting last-minute instructions before jumping out of the plane over Normandy on D-Day. I agreed. Who am I to judge BB? Who am I—a rich (by Filipino standards), spoiled brat American—to judge this kid trying to survive from day to day on the streets of Angeles City.

I took my tongue lashing. I was scared and going into a mild panic. I ordered myself to calm down. Then I asked, "Tell me about these bosses. Who are these guys?"

"These are all the local big deals, local politicians, shop owners, bar owners, police, and probably even a few GIs. You don't go against them, or it's curtains. It's funny to watch them attend ceremonies here on base, smiling, laughing, and joking with the base commander. These guys are ripping off the base commander blind, and yet they all hang out together like long-lost friends. It's entertaining to watch."

"What about BB? Where are his parents? How did he end up on the streets of Angeles City?"

"Story is that his parents sent him off to live with an uncle here. The parents promised to send money, but they never did. The uncle didn't want an extra mouth to feed, so out on the streets went BB. His story is pretty common. There are lots of street kids, left alone, abandoned. But somehow most of them make it. They can be extremely resourceful; do whatever it takes to survive.

"By the way, do you know how old BB is?"

"No," I answered, "I figured he's only about nine or ten. Do you know?"

Antonio finally gave me some good news. BB was older than I thought. "He's twelve. He looks younger, but he acts and thinks a lot older. I'd say he's go the smarts of a twenty-five-year-old. He can handle himself. You got nothing to feel bad about. Don't worry about BB; he'll be just fine."

My heart sunk. BB was a fighter. He was a tough guy, doing whatever it takes to survive on the streets. I felt low. I felt like a loser. I complained about the most mundane things, like ironing my uniform, polishing my shoes, or paying too much for a cup of coffee at the airport. And here's BB trying to survive from day to day on the streets of Angeles City, trying to figure out how to get food for the next meal, trying to figure out a safe place to lie down and sleep for the night.

I thought about BB's new market stall. I thought about how it was a much better place to spend the night than on the open street. I thought about what BB told me—how he insisted on staying in his new stall. He had such a proud tone in his voice, a tone of independence, a tone that told me and anyone listening, "I got this. Don't worry. I'm fine."

I held that thought as the conversation dropped off and my San Miguel drinking buddies started heading home. I held that thought as I lay in bed that evening trying to fall asleep. But my mind kept falling off the rails. My brain kept reminding me that BB was on the streets and I wasn't, that I was safe and he wasn't, that I was living the high life and he wasn't.

I finally drifted off to sleep because I couldn't fight off the "tired" anymore. Little did I know BB would have another in-your-face, bone-crushing, knee-wobbling, mind-numbing truth waiting for me the next day.

16. BACK TO BASE

I woke up early, very early. My body wanted more rest but my mind wouldn't have it. I kept thinking about BB on the streets of Angeles City. I tried to let his brave words comfort me, but it didn't work. He said he was OK. He said it's the best house he's ever had. He said he was used to living on the streets. Still, I felt awful. How could I leave him there? How cruel.

But I rationalized my position. "Hey, he's a tough kid; he'll be fine. What if I never came to the Philippines? He'd still be on the streets. I helped him out; I did a good deed."

I still felt guilty. I couldn't shake it.

"I know he's a twelve-year-old kid living on the streets. I don't care if he's got a street vendor stall. He's still on the streets. How could I—in good conscience—just leave him there?"

I got up before first light and took a cab to the main gate. From there I ran the couple hundred yards or so to the long row of market stalls and stopped at the first one—BB's.

I'd been thinking about what I wanted to tell him. I wanted to encourage him in his business, but I also wanted to talk to him about getting off the stolen cigarettes. Now that he's got some money, he can start buying from wholesalers—and get his business above board—no more illegal activity.

I also thought about my predicament. "Technically, I'm an accessory to the stolen cigarettes caper." I knew, and I didn't report it. I'd be in huge trouble if I got caught. But I figured the chances of getting caught were pretty slim. I did feel guilty about it, but not guilty enough to turn in BB. I made a promise to myself—"I won't do it." I could live with the guilt of being part of the crime. I couldn't live with the guilt of snitching on BB. Besides, I'd been warned by Antonio—snitching could very well be a non-habit-forming activity. Just like jumping out of an airplane at thirty thousand feet without a parachute—you only do it once.

Because of my predicament, I'd have to tell BB I can't hang around anymore. I'd have to steer clear of his stall and no longer have anything to do with his business. I was getting mentally prepared. I went over my speech in my head. I felt awful about it. But my "awful" was about to get much worse...

Upon arrival at BB's newly built stall, I wasn't ready for what I saw.

Reality got a lot more real.

As I looked into the stall past the opened flap, I saw BB holding a bowl of soupy white porridge in his left hand while his right hand was scooping out little portions and feeding it to the baby sitting in his lap.

I stopped cold. I didn't say a word. I tried to work out what I was witnessing. The baby was the same one I'd seen the day before lying between two pieces of cardboard. The little abandoned baby. I yelled to myself, "What's BB doing feeding the baby?"

I was praying for a guilt-free explanation—an explanation that would spare me more in-your-face reality. My prayers went unanswered.

BB calmly looked up and said, "Sean, this is my sister Irma. I got her some steamed rice from one of the ladies. She hasn't had rice in a few days, so this is going to be real good for her. She was sick, but she's getting better; this rice will cure her. I made enough money yesterday I could afford to get her some rice."

My jaw dropped until it hit the concrete street below. My eyes expanded to the size of a couple of manhole covers. My legs started wobbling; my mind started folding—I almost collapsed. I wish I'd worn a motorcycle helmet to soften the blow—ease the trauma from my head on collision with reality.

I did my best to collect myself. I had a big talk prepared—a talk about getting off the stolen cigarettes, finding another supplier, and making the operation legal. As I gathered my thoughts, I realized my talk would be the stupidest talk on the planet. It would be right up there with Marie Antoinette's famous talk: "Let them eat cake!" My talk was patronizing crap—rich kid condescending garbage. My talk would only make me look and feel like an idiot. I made a command decision—the talk got trashed, right into the incinerator, kicked to the back of my mind never to be heard from again.

My voiced cracked as I responded, "That's your sister? Why didn't you tell me you had a baby sister? Who else is with you?"

"It's just us. I was going to tell you, but we were so busy talking and setting up the stall, I forgot. Besides, when I tell people, they tend to think I'm going to beg for more money. So, I don't say anything. But now you know."

I stood there dumbfounded. BB continued.

"Mr. Sean, I've got to tell you something. You're my friend and I don't want to see you get in trouble. You helped me set up this stall, and I love it. My prayers have been answered. I've been praying for a house; then you came along, and now I've got one. Irma and I finally have a place of our own. You've been sent from God. So I don't want anything bad to happen to you."

I felt like I was getting a sermon from the Dalai Lama. BB sounded like a saint to me. "He's worried about my safety? He's worried about me?"

He kept talking.

"Some bad men came by the stall yesterday evening and wanted to know about you, why you're hanging around. They wanted to know your name and what we talked about. I told them I didn't know your name because we just met and we didn't talk about anything. They didn't believe me. They want to hurt you, Mr. Sean. I've seen what these guys do. You've got to get away from here. Stay on base; don't go off base anymore. I don't want anything to happen to you."

BB was now helping me—helping me stay alive. Our roles had reversed. I began by helping him; now he became my guardian angel. This smart, resourceful Angeles City street kid was saving my life, and probably putting his own life in danger.

I wasn't about to lecture BB about selling "illegal" cigarettes. I wasn't about to scold him for operating a "dodgy" business. I wasn't about to launch into a sermon about the virtues of business integrity. We were way past that. BB and I were now on the same playing field; we were operating in basic-survival mode. He and his sister locked in a constant search for the next meal. And me— locked in a life and death real world cat and mouse game. I had to win. Otherwise, I'd be another missing GI statistic. My most pressing goal was to get off the open streets of Angeles City and get back to the safety of the base.

I looked down at BB. I watched as he scooped more soupy white rice from the bowl and gently fed it to his baby sister. Irma gummed the nutritious rice, swallowed it, and then licked her lips to get the extra bits. It was difficult for me to leave, and yet difficult for me to stay. I felt I was going to burst into tears, like I would explode. The scene before me was overwhelming—overwhelmingly sad.

I looked for words. I found some, but they fell short. It's all I could muster. I was too emotional to think straight.

"BB, you take care. I admire you. You're a fighter. You're tough. Tougher than anyone I've ever met. Keep up the fighting spirit, and never ever give up. Thank you for warning me. Thank you for saving my life. I'll always remember you."

My eyes watered up. I reached in my wallet and grabbed a handful of pesos and set the money down pushing it under BB's sandal. He smiled and whispered, "Maraming salamat," which means "many thanks" in Tagalog.

I whispered back, "Walang an uman," which translates as "It's nothing." And that was the truth. My money gesture seemed like nothing. I was going to leave BB and Irma in the streets of Angeles City, and to ease my conscience I slide over a thousand pesos or so. As if it's going to make me feel any better, as if it's going to ease my guilty conscience, as if it's going to make any difference.

I needed to get back on base immediately. My guilty conscience would have to wait. I also figured BB can make it. He somehow survived two years on the streets of Angeles City. If he can do that then he can do anything. Now he's got his very own market stall to live in...no more living on the open streets. And I noticed that's how the other stall operators did it—they all seemed to live in their stalls. So, apparently, living in a street market stall is a very respectable way to operate. And BB seemed very happy with the arrangement. I wasn't. I'd rather see him and his sister in a proper house living with their mom and dad as a happy family. But like my dad used to tell me, "Put in one hand what you want in life and in the other hand what you get in life ... see which hand fills up first!"

I turned and started walking briskly in a direct line back to the Clark Air Base main gate.

17. MAC FLIGHT LOTTERY

As I entered the barracks, Antonio jumped up and ran over to me. He spoke in a low hurried voice. "Sean, you need to get out of here now. They're looking for you. Some men were snooping around asking if you were staying here. They work on base but they also work for the bosses. They'll kill you for a lousy couple of hundred pesos, probably got a bounty on your head. We covered for you, told them we've never seen you, nobody like that here. We sent them off to check the local hotels. Get over to the MAC terminal, and see if you can get a plane out of here today. You're safer in the MAC terminal. Just stay there until you catch a flight. I'll give you a ride, get your stuff, let's go."

I paused momentarily trying to understand my predicament. I was stuck in a mind loop, "... this can't be happening ... this can't be real ..." I snapped out of my stunned condition, ran to my room, grabbed my duffel bag, and tossed in my gear. I ran back out and saw Antonio's car. The passenger back door was already open. He was ready at the wheel and called out, "Get in the back and stay down. I don't want anyone to see you. I don't want to take any chances."

On the short drive to the terminal we talked. I was focused and scared. I had no trouble listening and talking while lying down in the back seat.

"How do you know they want to hurt me?"

"When they come looking for you, it's never good. They mean business. The bosses must be afraid you'll start talking about BB selling stolen cigarettes, and it will lead back to them. Best way to deal with it is to get rid of you. They wouldn't do it here on base. They'll take you off base, then finish you off. I know. That's how they operate. It doesn't take much money to bump someone off here in the Philippines. Your life isn't worth much if somebody with power and money wants you dead. Apparently, they want you dead, and it's pretty cheap to carry out the order. You need to get off the island—the sooner the better."

I listened and shuddered. "How did I get into this mess? How did I go from being a good guy helping a street kid with his business to a fugitive running for his life?"

Antonio stopped the car. I jumped out, pulling my duffel bag, and then headed toward the MAC terminal. After a few paces, I stopped, turned my head, and looked back at Antonio. I thought, "He saved my life. He didn't have to, but he did. He could have turned me in. He could have had the men wait for me at the barracks. He could have been part of the trap to capture me and finish me off. But instead he's protecting me. He's helping me escape."

I wanted to say something. I wanted to thank him. I wanted to express my gratitude. But the words wouldn't come out. I could see him watching me struggle for words. He didn't wait. He wasn't interested in hearing any sentimental last words. He made it very clear when he grabbed the airwaves and yelled, "Go! Go! Go!"

I snapped out of my momentary paralysis and immediately turned my head away from the getaway car. I walked briskly into the terminal, found the nearest men's room and changed into my uniform. I reported to the airman in charge, showed my leave papers and signed up for the next flight out. The next flight was at noon—destination Hickam.

I sat on a hard wooden bench and waited. After all, I was now in a waiting game. Waiting gave me time to think. And that's when the full force of my situation came to light. "There's a team of men who want me silenced. They want me dead. I'm a fugitive. I'm running for my life. I'm escaping from Clark Air Base. This is nuts! Crazy! How did my little MAC flight adventure turn into such a nightmare?"

After several hours of boring MAC terminal time, I began to feel a little better, a little less scared. I thought about what Antonio said: "You're safer in the MAC terminal." My guard dropped slightly.

My biggest anxiety now was getting a flight. I watched as the terminal filled up with passengers. "I'll bet they all have a higher priority than me. I could be stuck here for days." I quickly scratched that thought from my head and replaced it with another— something I'd forgotten. I got up from my seat and dragged my duffel bag to the nearby on-base phone. I picked up the receiver and dialed the number written down on the crumbled piece of paper.

"Hello, this is Sean Mitchell. May I speak to Chrisa, please?"

"OK, would you deliver a message for me?"

"Tell her I had to leave early, get back to Denver. Something came up, and I've got to catch a MAC flight today."

"OK, thank you. Good-bye."

I regret not catching up with Chrisa. I never saw her or spoke to her again. I miss her.

* * *

"OK, I want everyone to listen carefully. I'll call your name once and only once. If you don't answer, I go to the next name on the list, and you'll miss the flight. So, I want you all to stop talking," explained the airman first class to the gathered mass of people waiting to catch the next MAC flight to Hickam Air Force Base in Hawaii. It was almost the same speech I'd heard back in Hawaii on the way out to the Philippines. I figured they just read it off a script.

The airman called out the names, and the lucky ones started forming up to board the aircraft. I became concerned as it felt like he was getting to the end, the cutoff point. He called a lot of people. The plane can only fit so many.

Flights to Hickam were like gold; they filled up fast. That was the scuttlebutt I'd heard while waiting. I stopped listening when I overheard someone say they've been waiting for three days! I didn't need these negative inputs. I had to think positive. I had to believe I was going to be on this flight to Hickam.

My positive thinking and belief strategy started taking some serious hits. I had the lowest space-available priority. Almost everyone else waiting was on morale leave. My ordinary-leave status put me near or at the bottom of the priority ladder. I started thinking about ways to stay undercover for the next few days. I felt the sweat run down the bridge of my nose. The air conditioning was working fine, but my body started overheating from fear, worry, not knowing, and not having a plan to deal with a delay in getting off the island.

Tension built as folks began to realize they weren't going to get on the flight. The lady next to me started crying. Her three small children started crying too. I overheard her talking to no one in particular, saying, "I've got to get on this flight. Please God, let me get on this flight."

The airman in charge spoke up, "OK, this is the last person we'll take today. Everyone else will have to wait for the next flight. Listen up."

There was a delay as the airman started shuffling papers. I was desperately hoping to be called. I had strange visions—like I was appearing before a judge, waiting to be told if I was going to live or die. The airman stopped shuffling and pointed to a spot on one of the papers.

"Here it is. Let's see; is there a Lieutenant Mitchell here?"

I stepped forward.

"OK, folks, that's it. Lieutenant Mitchell, you're our last passenger."

I listened to the collective groan of about a hundred people getting notified that they'd lost the MAC flight lottery—they didn't make it. I did. I won. The lady with the three children screamed a long drawn out "Ahhhhhh!" followed by sobbing cries. I didn't look back. I just walked forward and took my place at the end of the line to board the plane. I felt bad about winning the MAC flight lottery, but not bad enough to give up my seat. I knew I had to get off the island; in my case it was a matter of life and death. I chose life.

The C-141 engines roared. The massive aircraft started slowly rolling down the runway. It picked up speed. The nose tipped up. I listened carefully to the sound of the wheels as they rolled rapidly across the tarmac. I listened with the intensity of a musician trying to work out a complicated bass line by ear. I listened impatiently. I wanted to hear a particular sound. I felt once I heard this sound, I'd be OK. I could breathe easy. Then suddenly I heard it—the beautiful sound of the wheels making no sound. We were airborne. At that moment I let out a gasp and whispered to myself, "I made it."

THE END

Share your insights, reflections and feedback. Write a heartfelt review on amazon.com and/or goodreads.com

ABOUT THE AUTHOR

Dave Ives was born in Melrose, Massachusetts, and raised in Pelham, New Hampshire. He joined the air force in October 1981 and served as a medical-service specialist at Mather Air Force Base near Sacramento, California, for two and a half years. Then he attended Ohio State as a full-time engineering student under an active-duty commissioning program. He was commissioned as second lieutenant in June 1987 and assigned to Buckley Air National Guard Base just outside of Denver, Colorado.

Dave is now a full-time property investor and author. He currently resides in Alice Springs, Northern Territory, Australia.

For more about Dave, visit his website **ivesguy.com**.

Other books by Dave Ives:

**The Adventures of an Air Force Medic**

**Live Free or Die**

**Perception Is Reality**

**Yanks in the Outback**: A Story of Woomera, South Australia, the Joint Defense Facility Nurrungar (JDFN) and the First Gulf War.

**Working My BUT Off!** Reflections of a Property Investor.

Made in the USA
Columbia, SC
28 February 2023